Simon Bloom,

THE
GRAVITY
KEEPER

SIMON BLOOM,

THE
GRAVITY
KEEPER

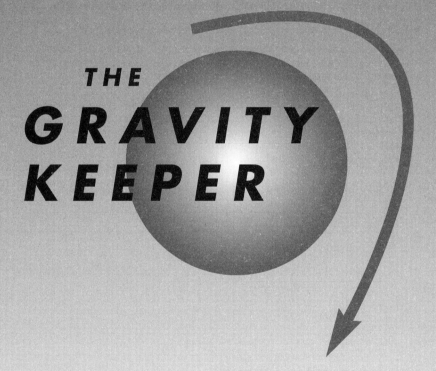

MICHAEL REISMAN

DUTTON CHILDREN'S BOOKS / WALDEN MEDIA

DUTTON CHILDREN'S BOOKS
A division of Penguin Young Readers Group

Published by the Penguin Group
Penguin Group (USA) Inc., 375 Hudson Street, New York, New York 10014, U.S.A.
Penguin Group (Canada), 90 Eglinton Avenue East, Suite 700, Toronto, Ontario, Canada M4P 2Y3 (a division of
Pearson Penguin Canada Inc.) • Penguin Books Ltd, 80 Strand, London WC2R 0RL, England • Penguin Ireland, 25
St Stephen's Green, Dublin 2, Ireland (a division of Penguin Books Ltd) • Penguin Group (Australia), 250
Camberwell Road, Camberwell, Victoria 3124, Australia (a division of Pearson Australia Group Pty Ltd) • Penguin
Books India Pvt Ltd, 11 Community Centre, Panchsheel Park, New Delhi – 110 017, India • Penguin Group (NZ),
67 Apollo Drive, Rosedale, North Shore 0632, New Zealand (a division of Pearson New Zealand Ltd) • Penguin
Books (South Africa) (Pty) Ltd, 24 Sturdee Avenue, Rosebank, Johannesburg 2196, South Africa • Penguin Books
Ltd, Registered Offices: 80 Strand, London WC2R 0RL, England

This book is published in partnership with Walden Media, LLC. Walden Media and the Walden
Media skipping stone logo are trademarks and registered trademarks of Walden Media, LLC,
294 Washington Street, Boston, MA 02108.

This book is a work of fiction. Names, characters, places, and incidents are either the product of
the author's imagination or are used fictitiously, and any resemblance to actual persons, living
or dead, business establishments, events, or locales is entirely coincidental.

The publisher does not have any control over and does not assume any responsibility for author
or third-party websites or their content.

CIP Data is available.

Published in the United States by Dutton Children's Books,
a division of Penguin Young Readers Group
345 Hudson Street, New York, New York 10014
www.penguin.com/youngreaders

Designed by Elizabeth Frances

Printed in USA   First Edition

ISBN 978-0-525-47922-2   10 9 8 7 6 5 4 3 2 1

This book is dedicated to my parents, without whom I wouldn't be here.

Acknowledgments

First, I want to applaud the late Douglas Adams, whose *The Hitchhiker's Guide to the Galaxy* really is my favorite book. I need to thank my mom, dad, grandma Elsie, sister Michele, and the rest of my family for moral, emotional, financial, and genetic support; Damon Ross for introductions and advice; my agent Nancy Gallt for her prowess and patience with me; Debbie Kovacs and Eloise Flood for my first book sale; supercool Margaret Wright for her aid in shaping my manuscript; and Mark McVeigh for shepherding the book to publication.

I am truly grateful for friends' reading and feedback: Yaniv; Jo and Angela; Ira; Laura, Jonathon, and Danielle; Julia; Larry; Stacy; Daniel; and more. Eternal thanks for wisdom, listening, and computer help, especially from Amir, Russ, Kenny, and Alison. Special gratitude goes to physics consultant Leigh, and to Lucia and the Insomnia Café gang for providing a great writing environment. I also want to acknowledge some teachers who showed me that school isn't all drudgery and number two pencils, most notably Mrs. Fenster and Ms. Brangan for encouraging and guiding my writing; and Mr. Friedman, Mr. Giglio, and Mr. Oliver for showing me that science can be fun. (Um, and if any of my former teachers think they recognize themselves . . . I hope they smile about it.)

Last but definitely not least, I want to thank everyone for reading this or, in fact any book (but especially this one)!

Simon Bloom,

THE
GRAVITY KEEPER

WELCOME TO MY CHRONICLE

Look around you. What do you see? If you're inside, you might see walls, carpeting, furniture. If you're outside, you might see grass, buildings, sky. But the world is a lot more complicated than it seems.

What do I mean? Here's an example: people. Most are just, well, people, but certain others are special. I'm one of those others. That person next to you could be, too, and you'd never know.

What makes us so special? The Books.

I'm not talking about the books you read for fun or for school or, in fact, anything you could buy in a store or find in a library. No, the books I mean are so important, they deserve a capital letter. They are called Books.

You see, everything around you—everything in the entire universe—has rules. Laws. And the Books contain the laws. Explain them. Control them. In ways that even I don't fully understand, the Books make sure the universe doesn't fall apart.

Those of us who know about the Books call ourselves the Union. We are the ones who, through the Books, keep the universe running smoothly (aside from occasional glitches like psychic visions or the way pens sometimes vanish when you're not looking).

Everyone else who's not in the Union is an Outsider— they don't know about the Books or understand how the universe works. Even Outsider scientists making discoveries, inventing things, and trying to explain why the sky is blue, how birds fly, or why chocolate tastes so good know only a small part of the truth.

The Union has always been somewhere behind the scenes, secretly watching over the Outsiders throughout history as they progress and evolve. Many pose as instructors— often professors or teachers—to better keep an eye on the Outsiders.

Nobody, not even those of us in the Union, knows where the Books come from or what they really are. Several of us, and I'm one of them, are convinced that the Books are living, thinking beings that actually had a hand, so to speak, in creating the universe. We believe the Books are to be respected, cared for, and even propped up in front of the television when there's a good show on.

Everyone in the Union agrees that the Books must be kept secret: with all the power they contain, the Books have the potential to be the most dangerous things in existence.

Why am I telling you all this? Because of my job—I'm a Narrator. I see what others see, hear what they hear, feel what they feel, and put it all in a Chronicle. But like all Narrators, I'm not allowed to interfere. This particular Chronicle is the story of how a magnificent and potentially devastating Book came into the hands of an eleven-year-old boy named Simon Bloom and how he changed the universe forever.

CHAPTER 1

SIMON BLOOM FEELS THE BREEZE

Simon Bloom lived in the northeastern part of the United States, in the northeastern part of New Jersey, in the northeastern part of Bergen County, in the northeastern part of Lawnville. His bedroom faced south.

His two-level house was on Jerome Street, a small road that ended a few houses down, turned a corner, and became the dead end Van Silas Way. Simon also lived a few blocks from Martin Van Buren Elementary, an ordinary school for students in kindergarten through sixth grade.

Simon looked ordinary, too. He had light brown hair, a light sprinkling of freckles on his average-size nose (which had a slight but unspectacular bump in the middle), and wide blue eyes. He was average height for his age but, much to his dismay, was one of the youngest in the sixth grade: he wouldn't be winning any tallness awards.

On what seemed to be a perfectly normal Sunday, Simon was flying. He soared through the air over Lawnville and did a loop-the-loop. He laughed as he felt the wind wash over him—laughing because, let's be honest, anyone who can fly and do a loop-the-loop without being strapped into a fancy jet plane has a reason to be in a good mood.

Simon then hovered in midair and concentrated. His body vibrated and changed color, turning from pinkish peach to a yellowish red, then to blue and finally, searing white. Then he exploded in a brilliant burst of blinding light. Tiny, glowing Simon particles scattered across the sky like a human firecracker. Unlike most fireworks, these embers regrouped and turned back into their normal Simon shape.

Next, Simon gazed at the daytime outline of the moon and concentrated again. He disappeared, instantly trans- porting himself from Lawnville and reappearing on the moon's barren, airless surface. There he gleefully jumped about and ran around, leaving footprints all across the dusty moonscape. After a moment, he looked around and sighed at how empty it was. This wasn't much fun without anyone joining in.

It was then that Simon Bloom felt a tug inside. He glanced at the Earth and blinked, transporting himself back to his bedroom. Where he was sitting at his desk chair, his eyes closed, imagining all this.

Yes, it's true: Simon only did those amazing things in his head. His was a very energetic mind. He was probably as active mentally as most professional athletes are physically, but Simon was a lot less likely to have his picture on a cereal box.

Actually, he hadn't left the house all morning, even though it was a beautiful day outside. His parents weren't home to urge him to go outside and enjoy the weather; both had gone into their offices to catch up on some work. Even when they were home, they were usually reviewing charts or notes.

His mother, Sylvia Bloom, was a high-powered advertising executive. She wore tailored business suits and tended to ask questions without waiting for the answer. His father, Steven Bloom, was an astrophysicist; he was completely obsessed with studying the universe. Sylvia often joked that Steven wouldn't notice a bomb going off near him, but that wasn't true: he'd probably study the nature of the explosion.

Simon didn't mind having workaholic parents. He kept to himself at home, at school, and everywhere in between. He was used to being ignored: his grades were good enough for his teachers to leave him alone, and he usually escaped notice from the bullies, too.

Sitting in his desk chair, Simon opened his eyes and

wondered where that weird tugging feeling had come from. He glanced around his room, looking over shelves and shelves of books, comics, and old toys: cars, spaceships, dinosaurs, superheroes, you name it. There were movie posters (mostly science fiction and fantasy), pictures of astronauts doing a spacewalk outside their space shuttle and bouncing on the moon, and a drawing by his all-time favorite artist, M. C. Escher.

Escher drew the impossible—the rules of reality bending in crazy ways. The one on Simon's wall was called *Relativity*. It was the inside of a house with people walking up different stairways set at every angle. Some people were completely upside down in relation to others, but each person walked as if his was the normal stairway.

Simon looked at the book he'd been reading earlier: *The Hitchhiker's Guide to the Galaxy*, by Douglas Adams. It was his favorite book, about a perfectly ordinary British man named Arthur Dent who goes with a group of aliens on an incredible adventure throughout the galaxy. Simon loved it because he wished he was Arthur.

But that book wasn't the source of the tugging, nor was the Escher picture. It was something outside his window. Simon opened it, and that's when he felt a breeze. No, the Breeze. Like the Books, it was important enough for the big *B*.

You see, this was not a normal puff of wind. It was soothing and exciting as it washed over Simon. It made him tingle with thoughts and possibilities. It gave him the tiniest glimpse of a special, hidden part of the world. For a moment, he felt like he really was flying, really was a dazzling firework, really was teleporting to the moon . . . and more. Like he could do anything and anything could happen.

The Breeze faded away and Simon turned back to his room. But he didn't—he couldn't—forget that feeling.

CHAPTER 2

A Change in the Weather

It was Sunday. Some religions view Sunday as a holy day. Many people consider Sunday a day of rest on which nobody should do anything but relax, watch sports, ride bicycles, bake muffins, or hurl wires with hooks at swimming fish.

For most Union members, Sunday was a time for important meetings that the Outsiders knew nothing about. For those in my Society, it was a time to watch these meetings closely. And for the Union members that I watched, Sundays required raincoats.

Although most of Lawnville, New Jersey, was experiencing a beautiful May day, around the corner from Simon Bloom's house it was another matter entirely. It was raining there on quiet, dead-end Van Silas Way. Raining hard. The expression "cats and dogs" didn't cover it; "tigers and wolves" was more accurate. The downpour was so fierce that the residents of Van Silas Way huddled in their nice, dry houses, unwilling to leave or even look out their windows.

In the middle of the soaking-wet road, a glowing blue dot appeared. The dot stretched into a ten-foot-long line, which grew upward, silently forming a ten-foot-high wall. Though ten feet high and ten feet wide, the wall was paper thin; if viewed from the side, it would be nearly invisible. (Of course, nobody could see much with that amount of rain anyway, but I thought I'd mention it.)

The wall was a type of door, known as a Gateway, which many in the Union use for traveling distances in seconds without having to deal with speeding tickets, shuttle launches, or airplane food.

One by one, a group of people stepped out of the glowing blue Gateway and into the soaked street. Their hooded raincoats shielded them from the rain, but they were still cold and damp as they trudged along the water-drenched street. One chewed delicious strawberry gum, but the rain washed it away when he tried blowing a bubble.

(I felt sorry for them . . . I was warm and dry and happily chewed my own gum. It was grape.)

As they reached the end of the street and stepped into Dunkerhook Woods, they sighed in relief. This was the sacred meeting place of their Order, and it was perfectly dry.

Outside weather was not allowed in Dunkerhook Woods.

Clouds could hover outside and pout about it as much as they liked, but not a single drop of wet ever entered the area. You could ask why the forest didn't simply dry up and die, but it would be a silly question. Any forest that was able to keep rain away could be trusted to have its own method of staying healthy.

Once the last person entered the woods, the glowing blue Gateway sank back into the ground, shrank into a line again, then a dot, and disappeared. The rain stopped, as if a faucet had been shut off; with the Gateway gone, it wasn't needed.

As the raincoat-wearing people shuffled along the main pathway into the woods, the Breeze blew over them. It dried the moisture from the rain and soothed their jangled nerves, leaving them feeling wonderfully refreshed, even tingly. The people tossed back their hoods and savored the clean air.

No one noticed that one man, dressed in a faded tan hooded overcoat and walking with a cane, absently veered off the path. He stumbled around through the trees and shrubs as the others walked on. There was nobody else around him in the forest when he fell, but philosophers should note that he still made a sound. (It was a rather annoyed swearword, but it counted.)

That man's name was Ralfagon Wintrofline.

The rest of the group followed the trail into a huge open space with many thick, smooth-topped tree stumps. The stumps were arranged so they faced a single, taller stump on the opposite side of the clearing. This was an important place for these people. Its official name was The Grand Meeting Place Where the Order Shall Convene, Contemplate, Converse, Control, and Sit on Tree Stumps, but most just called it the clearing.

Each person settled comfortably onto a stump. That might sound unlikely, given that tree stumps are made of wood and are thus normally hard, flat, and only good for giving out splinters, but these were no ordinary tree stumps. They were quite spongy and comfy, like sitting on a nicely padded chair. They didn't recline or anything, but they were rather impressive for a forest.

It was several more moments before Ralfagon Wintrofline appeared. Actually, *appeared* is too dramatic a description: he slowly limped out of a cluster of bushes over to the tallest stump. He lowered himself carefully to his seat and then slumped forward.

As he pulled back his rain hood, he did not appear important, much less intimidating. His crinkled skin, unevenly cut gray hair, fuzzy gray eyebrows, and blurry gray eyes made him look confused. He slouched when he sat and stooped when he walked, using a scratched-up wooden cane with a shiny handle.

That cane (a gift from an old friend who no longer lived on the planet) was the first sign that Ralfagon was more than he seemed. The oval handle, made of a unique metal, contained a highly detailed—though minuscule—map of the Milky Way galaxy. It was accurate to the last moon, and whenever something in the galaxy changed, so did the handle.

Impressive or not, Ralfagon was the leader of this group. They were the Order of Physics, and he was known as their Keeper. And so Ralfagon Wintrofline, one of the most powerful men in the universe, had a meeting to begin. He cleared his throat, sat up straight, and stuck a finger in his ear.

The Order members waited while he rummaged around in there; he did this every Sunday. "Does anybody have a cotton swab?" he asked in a crackly voice. "The Breeze never dries the insides of my ears." Almost everyone produced a swab, and he chose one. "Isn't that rain wet?" he asked as he tended to his moist ear canal.

Nobody answered, but he didn't notice. Ralfagon Wintrofline was known for his rhetorical questions.

"Much better," he said after a moment. "Shall we proceed?" He paused, knowing there was something important he had to do . . . if he could only remember what. "Er, Eldonna, could you come here, please?"

Short, stout Eldonna Pombina walked over and whispered in his ear. "Here are your notes, sir," she said as she handed him a handful of pages.

"Notes? Why would I need . . . Oh, of course. Thank you."

Eldonna nodded, unbothered by his forgetfulness. Ralfagon Wintrofline was known as Professor Ralph Winter to his colleagues at nearby Milnes University, a small, charming university famed throughout all of north Jersey for its excellent vending machines. There, Eldonna Pombina called herself Donna Pom and worked as Professor Winter's teaching assistant.

She handled most questions from students in Ralfagon's physics classes. She also made sure he could find his classroom and, when the day was done, his way home.

Ralfagon turned and shuffled the notes until he found what he wanted. "Ah, yes. Right. Meeting. Very serious." He looked up at the Order members. "And that's why we're here today, through the rain. I'll see if I can put an end to that wretched downpour."

Willoughby Wanderby thrust his hand up from his stump seat. He was a middle-size man of middling years with middle-of-the-road features, yet there was something hard about him. He had the sort of stern, forceful manner of a military commander, a world leader, or perhaps a gym teacher. "But Ralfagon, the rain has a purpose—it hides our comings and goings from Outsiders."

Ralfagon nodded sagely. "Right. So. I'll keep that going until we stop meeting then, yes? Good. Where was I? Ah, this meeting. I'm afraid it will be our last. Hmm, that takes care of the rain."

The other members of the Order of Physics spent several minutes sputtering in shock while Ralfagon calmly swabbed his other ear. He found it very satisfying.

TIME-OUT

What was happening? First an Outsider boy appeared so prominently in my Chronicle and now the Order of Physics was coming to an end? This had never happened before, not in the entire history of the Union. And I, of all people, should know—history is my job!

What could this mean? What disasters would it lead to?

Would the universe fall into chaos without the Order of Physics to maintain it? Would the Outsider scientists flounder helplessly without the subtle guidance provided by the Order? Would all of humanity plunge back into the Dark Ages? More importantly, would I need to find a new job? Would I get stuck Narrating nature shows?

My fabled calm was shattered. Something had to be done. I decided to take action in the manner of all Narrators: I popped another piece of gum into my mouth and resumed watching, ready for further action (if necessary).

CHAPTER 3

THE POWERS THAT BE

The Order was still murmuring in confusion when a very tall member on a back-row stump leapt to his feet. Mermon Veenie.

Mermon's dark hair was slicked back, framing a wide forehead and sharply angled eyebrows. Beneath those were teeny-tiny eyes that looked like black dots drawn in with a Magic Marker rather than things that could be used for seeing. But Mermon seemed to have no trouble glaring at Ralfagon.

He spoke in a loud, growling voice that made you think he might go for your throat after he finished speaking. Or, if he was in a bad mood, while he was midsentence. "Old man, what are you talking about?" he snarled.

Most of the Order members frowned at Mermon's disrespect; Ralfagon merely raised a finger. "Please sit down, Mermon," he said calmly, "and I'll explain."

"Maybe *you* shouldn't be leading this group!" Mermon growled. "I, for one, am tired of your nonsense; maybe it's time I did something about it!" As he spoke Mermon shook a fist at his leader; sparks literally jumped from his knuckles. The Order members seated around him leaned away on their stumps.

Ralfagon's placid expression changed to a grimace, and though he barely moved, he no longer seemed as stooped and frail. The corner of a thick blue Book peeked out from his overcoat, and the woods crackled with power.

Ralfagon said a series of unintelligible words that sounded like he was speaking backward and forward at the same time while chewing peanut butter. There was nothing peanut buttery involved, however; no, Ralfagon was invoking a formula—he was controlling a law of physics.

Mermon tried to respond but could only flap his mouth uselessly: Ralfagon had taken away his ability to make sound. The Order members all gasped loudly (except for Mermon, who couldn't).

Next, Ralfagon quickly spoke several other formulas and gestured with his finger. Mermon was flung back ten feet from the group and launched high in the air with the speed of a cannonball. He jolted to a halt far above the clearing and hung there, waving his hands helplessly. He was then spun around and around like a Mermon-shaped top. He stopped abruptly and plummeted even faster than he'd risen; he screamed silently and flailed his limbs all the way down.

Ralfagon snapped his fingers and Mermon stopped instantly, all his momentum gone. He was stretched out so close to the dirt that a passing ant's antennae brushed against his nose. (The ant just kept on walking; like most creatures in the woods, it had learned to ignore the Order's activities.) Ralfagon wiggled his finger, and Mermon returned to his feet in the exact position he'd been in before. His once-neat black hair was sticking straight up, and his wide mouth quivered as if he was unsure whether to throw up, burst out crying, or do both at once.

"I have told you before, Mermon," Ralfagon said quietly but sternly, "I will not tolerate threats to myself or any other Order member. Now, take your seat and behave yourself."

Mermon dropped down onto his stump and lowered his head in penitence.

Ralfagon spoke his first formula in reverse, returning Mermon's ability to speak. He then relaxed back into his usual slouch. "As I was saying, we will be stopping our meetings. For a time. This is not *my* decision. The Council of Sciences had our weekly meeting earlier today; we had a special visitor." He frowned. "An official from the Board of Administration came with complaints, several aimed at our

Order. We were congratulated on our fix of the Bermuda Triangle, but he raised other issues, such as the Atlantis fiasco. The yeti. Forty-two separate incidences of Slinkys not making it all the way down sets of stairs."

Willoughby Wanderby raised his hand and, at Ralfagon's nod, said, "I'm confused. Atlantis sank many centuries ago; surely that's not relevant now? And the yeti . . . you mean Abominable Snowmen? If anything, those beasts are the Order of Biology's mix-up."

Ralfagon sighed. "Nobody's forgotten Atlantis. I keep getting Time-Life books about it; the shipping and handling alone is outrageous. As for the yeti, Biology's Keeper, Gilio Skidowsa, claims they're due to the electromagnetic flux of the northern lights. I just see it as a marketing problem; what do you expect when you call something *Abominable?*" He sighed again. "The Board official suspended all Science Order activities until a plan can be made to fix things."

One of the younger Order members, a pretty woman with red hair, shook her head. "Bureaucratic nonsense. Does that mean we can't do any work today?"

Ralfagon scratched his wrinkled chin. "No, Loisana, I think we can have one last session. Something quick and easy. Let's boost mobile phone radiation. We all could use the better phone reception, and it'll certainly cheer up the Outsiders."

Ralfagon leaned his cane against his stump and gestured, triggering the same powers he'd used to send Mermon hurtling through the air. Now, however, Ralfagon levitated gently until he was standing atop his stump. The other Order members rose from their seats and linked their hands in a circle around him.

Ralfagon raised his hands in the air and wiggled his fingers. The blue Book slid out of his coat, but instead of falling to the ground as any self-respecting, ordinary book would do, it floated to just above Ralfagon's fingertips.

The others each spoke their own formulas, activating the various laws of physics they commanded. Rather than use this control, they simply combined their energy and willpower with Ralfagon's. Their circle glowed blue, and under Ralfagon's guidance, their influence spread quickly across the globe and strengthened mobile phones' signal strength.

All the Order members' eyes were closed, so they couldn't see what I saw: a figure, walking just outside their circle, outlined in the blue light. His coat had an oversize hood that hid his face entirely as he moved toward Ralfagon. He came too close as he passed behind a burly man with dark brown skin and thick eyeglasses; a ripple formed in the blue glow between them.

That ripple disrupted the bespectacled man's concentration and triggered his formula: a fierce rumble rolled out from behind him as the ground shook. Everyone dropped their hands and opened their eyes, but when the blue glow faded, the hooded figure mysteriously vanished. I was the only one who'd seen him.

The Book dropped into Ralfagon's fingers. "Robertitus?"

Robertitus Charlsus groaned and adjusted his glasses. "I'm sorry, Ralfagon. I couldn't help myself."

"It's not your fault," Ralfagon said. "Something disrupted our circle."

Everyone looked at Mermon Veenie, who shook his head. "I didn't do anything! I swear!"

Loisana pointed into the distance. "Look at the path!"

There was a jagged tear across the trail a few hundred yards from the clearing; the chasm was at least forty feet across.

"It's fine," Ralfagon said, but he frowned. "We never enter on that side of the clearing. Besides, Dunkerhook Woods takes care of itself. By the time we resume our meetings, the damage will probably be gone."

The Order members milled about; they discussed possible vacation plans and bemoaned now–useless supplies of cotton swabs. They all lived in town, so they'd see plenty of one another, but there was still an air of sadness.

Mermon stood apart. He glowered briefly at Ralfagon and then stared off into the clearing, as if searching for something . . . or someone.

Eventually, the Order members zipped up their raincoats, tugged on their hoods, and marched down the trail toward the border of Van Silas Way. Ralfagon was still frowning and looking vaguely puzzled. The rain started again on the street, the Gateway reappeared, and one by one, the Order members filed through and went on home.

Nobody noticed that Mermon Veenie lingered in the woods, standing off to the side behind a tree. "Sir? Are you there?" he said once the others had left.

"Veenie, you moron." A toneless, echoing voice boomed out of the empty air, as if somebody was shouting into a large, invisible bucket. **"What if they notice you didn't leave? If one of them came back, they'd hear and thus be able to see me."**

As the words rang out, the speaker became visible—it was the hooded figure. He was completely covered by a black coat; his hood covered his head like a huge, shadowed cave. There was no sign of a face.

For the second time that day, Mermon had to apologize. "I'm sorry, sir. I was worried. Won't the Order disbanding ruin our plans?"

The hooded head shook from side to side. **"Exactly the opposite. This is all part of *my* plan. In a few more days, we will strike. Then we will have the power, and I will have my revenge. But no more nonsense like threatening Ralfagon. Control your bad judg-ment from now on and await my signal. Now go."**

Mermon Veenie nodded and left through the waiting Gateway. The hooded figure disappeared. Soon after, the Gateway vanished, the rain stopped, and all was quiet in the woods once again.

CHAPTER 4

A MATTER OF PRINCIPAL

The next day was Monday, and that meant school for Simon. He daydreamed as he walked the few blocks between home and Martin Van Buren Elementary, heading for the back entrance. He passed through the school's large, fenced-in playground where children in the lower grades frolicked.

He paid little mind to the joyous screams and laughs made by younger kids climbing on the large metal jungle gym or playing with the swings, seesaws, and rings. He glanced at the rings: those five-foot-high, four-foot-wide concrete tubes always made Simon think of giant toilet paper rolls turned on their sides, except these were concrete, embedded in the ground, and had no toilet paper on them.

Simon went through the double doors and into the hall-way, noting the change in sound. While the playground was alive with squeals of childish pleasure, the school halls were filled with a steady beat of noise. The boys were mostly roughhousing or shouting to one another while many of the girls stood around in clumps, chatting about clothes, televi-sion shows, and even boys.

Simon concentrated on shutting himself off from all that activity, tuning out the sights and sounds. He pressed through the mass of moving kids and squeezed free to his locker, where he started absently emptying his backpack into his locker. A tap on the shoulder startled him.

"You dropped this."

Simon was jolted back to the world around him. He turned and saw Alysha Davis, whose locker was next to his. She had coffee-and-cream-colored skin and long, wavy brown hair tied back in a ponytail. As he looked up (she was taller than he), all he could think to say was, "Huh?"

Alysha gestured with a paperback book in one hand. "This fell out of your backpack. You feeling okay?"

Simon saw what was in her hand: *The Hitchhiker's Guide to the Galaxy*. He'd mistakenly packed it with his schoolbooks. "Yeah. Thanks."

Alysha handed it to him. "Wasn't that a movie?" she asked, raising her voice to be heard over a scratchy, almost incomprehensible announcement coming from the PA system. Simon nodded. She pointed to the words on the cover. "'Don't panic'? What does *that* mean?"

Simon was suddenly embarrassed, wondering what she would think of the stuff he read. He mustered a half smile and shrugged. "It means 'don't panic.'" He turned and stuffed the book into his locker.

He could feel Alysha looking at him, but he didn't turn around. What else was he supposed to say? They'd been friends years ago, but now she was popular and hung out with kids who wouldn't even look at him. Fashion had somehow become a big thing for her; her new friends judged one another—and everyone else—by the clothes they wore and how they looked in them. It was a world Simon didn't understand or want to enter.

Simon was saved, in a way, by a bump from behind. He almost fell into his locker as Marcus Van Ny brushed past him to talk to Alysha.

"'Scuse me, Sam, didn't see you there," Marcus said without looking at him. "Hey, Allie, you going to Nezzo's after school today?"

Simon hurried to get his books and go; he didn't want to risk making Marcus angry. Tall and athletic Marcus Van Ny was one of the most popular kids in the sixth grade; even the teachers loved him. They saw his wide, gleaming smile, his glossy black hair, and his perfect grades and thought he was an angel.

In truth, Marcus was feared by most sixth graders. He'd never lost a fight, but he mostly left the rough stuff to his best friend, Barry Stern. Barry wasn't as smart or handsome as Marcus, but he was so big he could have passed for a ninth grader. Plus, he was fiercely loyal to Marcus. Marcus gave him desserts at lunchtime, fed him answers in class, and brought him along to parties. In return, Barry pummeled anyone that Marcus didn't want to be bothered with.

Simon closed his locker and quickly slipped away, merging into the hallway traffic. He rushed into the classroom, noting that he was the first student there: the other kids were out in the halls with their friends. The teacher wasn't there, either. She must have just stepped out: a mug of coffee steamed on her desk and bits of chalk dust still floated in the air from a message on the board: TAKE YOUR SEATS.

Simon sat down at his desk in the back of the classroom, far from the clatter outside. He looked up at the ceiling and let his mind wander off; he was imagining a tiny race of people living in the glass-covered space around the fluorescent lights when a loud clacking jarred him from his thoughts. Class was already under way and his teacher, Mrs. Desmond, was smacking her wooden pointer against the blackboard to get everybody's attention.

Simon looked next to his short, wrinkled teacher and saw a giant.

Okay, not a giant. She was just under six feet tall in her heeled shoes, but her hair made her seem much taller. From the scalp down, she wasn't that unusual—she had a pleasant face; a small but comforting smile; thick, black-framed glasses; and a simple beige pantsuit. She held a slim leather briefcase. Perfectly normal.

The top of her head was a different story. She had the most amazing stack of jet-black hair that extended over two feet straight up. Remarkably, this tower didn't jiggle when she moved her head. It was like stone. Simon didn't know much about hair spray, but he wondered how so much hair could possibly keep from wobbling.

As he stared at it, the upper few inches of the hair bent forward.

Simon held back a gasp as that topmost portion practically folded over and, it seemed, started to swivel around. He supposed her hair spray had given out or something.

"Class, this is our new principal," Mrs. Desmond said. "Miss . . . Fanstrom, is it?"

Miss Fanstrom nodded, and aside from that moving top part, her hair still didn't wiggle. Suddenly, that top section stopped, angled at one spot, as if pointing. It was aimed right at Simon.

Mrs. Desmond continued, "Mr. Shimshamp was suddenly called away for, er, how long, Miss Fanstrom?"

Miss Fanstrom smiled. "Indefinitely, it seems." She had a crisp English accent that, Simon thought, made her sound very sophisticated. "I'm afraid you're stuck with me for quite a while," she said with a slight smile. "I'm told he was offered a top position in a distant college's history department. Apparently they made him an offer he couldn't refuse."

Mrs. Desmond's forehead scrunched in confusion. "Oh. I see. This happened on a Sunday?" she asked Miss Fanstrom. "With less than a month left in the school year? And . . . the school board was able to find you on such short notice?"

Miss Fanstrom turned to face the teacher directly, but that top part of her hair flopped over so it seemed to keep pointing at Simon. "Fortunate, isn't it? In my line of work, it is best to be ready for emergencies." She again gave a small smile and cleared her throat, bringing the teacher out of her surprised state. "Mrs. Desmond," she whispered, "the class? My guide?"

"Oh yes," Mrs. Desmond said, giving a long look at Miss Fanstrom's hair before turning back to the class. "As I was saying, Miss Fanstrom is your new principal. I expect there'll be a school-wide assembly later so she can officially introduce herself, but right now . . ." She glanced back at Miss Fanstrom, who gave her an encouraging nod. "Right now she'd like one of you to show her around the school."

Miss Fanstrom turned to face the sixth graders and smiled. "Yes. My office is being fixed up by some workmen. Minor adjustments here and there. A perfect time for one of you to give me a tour; I'd hate to get lost on my first day."

Mrs. Desmond beamed as she gestured toward Marcus in the back row; he was the one student whose gaze wasn't locked on Miss Fanstrom's column of hair. He was looking at

Alysha, who sat a few rows ahead of him. When he noticed Mrs. Desmond looking his way, he snapped to attention and flashed his patented grin.

"May I suggest Marcus Van Ny," the teacher said. "He's our top student and a fine athlete, so he should be—"

Miss Fanstrom's voice didn't waver, but her smile slipped a bit when she heard Marcus's name. She cut Mrs. Desmond off with a quick slash of her hand. "No, thank you. I'm sure Mr. Van Ny is quite capable, but I was thinking of someone else. Perhaps . . ." She made a show of turning her head from side to side, as if searching the room, but Simon noted that her eyes (and the top of her hair) never left him. "That young man."

Mrs. Desmond squinted to follow Miss Fanstrom's pointed finger. "Him? Er, Stanley? No, my mistake, Simon. Simon Bloom. But he—" She stopped herself. "Of course, Miss Fanstrom. Simon, would you mind?"

Simon rose from his seat, his mind bubbling with questions, but he just nodded and followed Miss Fanstrom—and her strange hairdo—out the door.

CHAPTER 5

SIMON FOLLOWS THE BREEZE, OWEN MEETS THE TREES

Simon trotted alongside Miss Fanstrom, who swung her briefcase as she walked. Minutes stretched by with neither saying a word. The halls were a different place during classtime; there was no noise but the squeaking of his sneakers and the clunking of her heeled shoes on the tiled floor. Simon had started to wonder if she'd forgotten about him when she asked, "So, Mr. Bloom, how are you enjoying your school experience?"

"It's okay," Simon said.

Miss Fanstrom chuckled. "My, how descriptive. Any subjects you like?"

Simon thought for a moment. "I like reading. And science is all right."

Miss Fanstrom nodded. Simon noticed that the top of her hair was still bent toward him, but when he looked directly at it, it seemed to pop back up again. Simon shook his head, not sure whether he'd imagined it.

"Reading: always a good thing," Miss Fanstrom said. "And science; like father, like son, yes?"

Simon gaped. "My . . . father? How did you—?"

"I've had time to examine a few of the students' files."

Simon just blinked and hurried to follow her out the exit to the playground. For some reason, Miss Fanstrom turned to the brick wall on the left, which faced out into the playground, and nodded. She reached out and knocked against it. "Well done," she murmured. "Blends right in."

Before Simon could ask her what she meant, she turned back to the school.

"Mr. Bloom, do you know the way to my office?"

"Yes, Miss Fanstrom."

"But not from personal experience, eh? Like to keep your nose clean, so I see. That's good. Science is a fine subject, Mr. Bloom. Just watch yourself, dear boy. There are other dangers to watch for besides tough fellows roaming the halls. Keep alert outside the school, but also inside. Ah, here we are!"

They'd arrived at her office. Simon wondered what use the tour had been; they'd barely explored the first floor, much less the whole school. Before Simon could ask, he noticed the two workers in Miss Fanstrom's office.

They were dressed in denim overalls covered with pockets practically overflowing with tools. Simon saw rulers, compasses, pencils, X-Acto knives, and screwdrivers poking out. But there were also coiled wires, circuitry boards, and strange fixtures that he didn't recognize. On the floor was a large toolbox filled with more tools, many unlike anything he'd ever seen. Both workers wore caps with the word *Guild* neatly embroidered on the front.

One worker was up a ladder at the top of the doorway. Simon noted a piece had been cut out of the wall to make the doorway extra high, probably to accommodate Miss Fanstrom's hair. He gawked at a beige metal box with wires, tubes, and even a small compass coming out of it that the worker was installing just above the expanded doorway.

Miss Fanstrom entered her office and pulled a fancy gray notebook computer out of her briefcase. She placed it on her desk, and Simon stared at it; it looked sturdy, like it was made of solid metal.

"Thank you, Mr. Bloom. This has been a lovely tour; an honor, really. Please return to class and tell Mrs. Desmond that yours was a job well done."

Simon looked back to Miss Fanstrom. That was it? He said good-bye and walked back to class.

For the rest of the morning, Miss Fanstrom's hair and the tour gave him plenty to ponder. He wondered what she had meant about science. And about danger? Besides, how odd was it that Mr. Shimshamp quit suddenly and a new principal got hired the very next day? She seemed nice, but was that just a cover? And if it was—a cover for what?

Simon was jolted from his thoughts by the lunchtime bell. He waited until the streams of kids were gone from the halls so he could avoid the bumping and pushing. He got his lunch box from his locker without seeing a single classmate.

The peace was broken by the distant sound of a door slamming, followed by a yelp of fear; Simon turned and, moments later, saw Owen Walters rush past toward the staircase at the end of the hall. Fearing the worst, Simon ran, too; he didn't want to meet whoever was chasing Owen.

Simon found the boy cowering against the wall at the bottom of the stairs, with his arms crossed in front of his face. "Please–I'm–sorry–I–spilled–your–lunch–on–you–I–promise–I–won't–do–it–again–just–leave–me–alone!"

Simon, as always, was impressed that Owen could say so much without taking a breath. "Owen, what are you doing?"

Owen lowered his arms and tried to calm down. "Oh, it's you, Simon. But where are they?"

"Who?" Simon looked around.

"Marcus and Barry. They're after me, but it was an accident. It's not my fault I'm such a klutz!"

"You spilled Marcus's lunch on him?" Simon asked.

"And it's chili day," Owen moaned. "That stains, you know!"

Simon heard the boys' room door at the other end of the hall slam open; they'd probably just checked the stalls looking for Owen and would hit the stairwell next. "Come with me. Hurry up!"

He dragged Owen out the rear double doors and through the playground. They passed dozens of screaming, romping children.

Simon led Owen to a concrete tube at the far end of the playground; it had no kids in it, so they crouched inside. It was positioned such that a person would have to go right to the opening to see them. "Now keep quiet," he said. "They might not bother coming all the way out here to look for you."

Simon poked his head out of the end of the tube, staring past the ankles of the playing children. At the double doors, Marcus appeared. Simon couldn't see his face, but he recognized those brand-new, ultraexpensive sneakers—named after some basketball player that Simon couldn't remember—that nobody else in school owned. Those, plus a pair of pricey jeans that Simon's mother had once said cost a fortune, made Simon sure it was him. Only now the sneakers and jeans were covered in chili.

Simon watched Marcus scan the playground from the doorway. Cool kids, especially Marcus, avoided going out there among the sticky, clingy younger kids.

Finally, Marcus went inside, and Simon turned to Owen. "Coast's clear."

Owen was too busy panting with fear to respond. Simon wasn't close friends with Owen but had always thought he was nice enough. Owen was short for twelve (a few inches shorter than Simon), but that wasn't why the other kids picked on him. They did it because he made it so easy.

Owen was jumpy—he got scared by the smallest things. Fire drills, the bell at the start of the day, the bell at the end of the day. Clapping. Taco day in the school cafeteria (especially the shredded lettuce).

That's just the way he was. He wouldn't call a glass of water half full or half empty; he'd assume it was poisoned and run away.

"Thank–you–so–much," Owen finally gasped. "You–saved–my–life." When he was extra nervous, Owen also tended to speak without stopping, as if he was afraid to pause for air.

"Try breathing a little, okay?" Simon opened his lunch box and saw Owen looking at him with puppy dog eyes; he must have abandoned his own lunch when he ran. Simon sighed. "Want half a ham on rye and a cookie?"

At the end of the day, as Simon stood by his locker, gathering his homework, he saw Owen watching from around the corner. Fortunately Alysha wasn't there; Simon guessed Owen would have a heart attack if he saw any of Marcus's friends.

Once Simon had his books together, he walked toward the door where Owen was standing. Owen didn't say a word, but he had that puppy dog look again.

"You wanna walk with me?" Simon asked. Owen nodded, and they set out together. They walked in silence until they got close to Simon's house, where Simon suddenly got that tugging sensation and the inviting touch of the Breeze, just as he had on Sunday. "Do you feel that?"

Owen looked around in a panic. "Did–something–bite–you–or–sting–you?"

"No, Owen. Relax. It's just some wind. But it feels great . . . the best thing I've ever felt. It's coming from there." He pointed toward Van Silas Way as the Breeze coursed through him. "Let's check it out."

Owen sniffed the air. "Could–be–a–fire–or–the–power–lines–or–air–pollution." But he followed Simon anyway.

Small towns like Lawnville usually have someplace that people tell stories about, such as a haunted house, a cursed cul-de-sac, or a petrifying parking lot. Often, kids in those towns dare other kids to run into the place and do something (knock on a door, write their name, bray like a donkey) to show how courageous they are.

Dunkerhook Woods was *not* one of those places. Nobody thought about going into the small forest at the dead end of Van Silas Way. Outsiders, young or old, simply didn't notice it. No car had ever mistakenly driven in, no loose ball had ever accidentally bounced in, no Frisbee had ever unintentionally sailed in.

In fact, if somebody was to really think about it, they'd

wonder if some power was working to hide Dunkerhook Woods. But such a power would also keep Outsiders from thinking that, and that's what it did.

The trees in Dunkerhook Woods were thick and high, many tall enough to rival the famed redwoods of the Pacific Northwest. But thanks to the very old, very effective safeguards that kept the place hidden, no Outsiders noticed the trees towering over all of Lawnville. People who lived in the areas nearest the woods noticed that their neighborhoods were often cooler, as if in the shade. Once again, those powerful forces surrounding the woods stopped people from dwelling on it. Thus, the Order's meeting place remained secret, and a great agricultural wonder of New Jersey went all but unnoticed.

As Simon and Owen reached Van Silas Way, Simon was disappointed: it was a regular, dull-looking street. He was about to turn away from the dead end, but the Breeze grew stronger. It wrapped itself around him and invigorated him. To Simon, it felt like an invitation.

While Owen saw nothing but a dead-end street, the lush, green woods appeared before Simon. "Wow," he said, "look at *that* place!"

Owen blinked. "What place?"

Simon pointed. "There, those woods with the gigantic trees! It looks . . . incredible. I guess I never noticed it somehow."

Owen squinted in confusion. The Breeze hadn't touched him, so he wasn't officially invited. "Maybe you need some rest, or you've caught the flu or something, but Simon, it's just a street."

Simon, naturally, thought Owen was afraid; how could he not see the woods, right there in front of them? "Come on," Simon said. "They're just big trees."

Simon strode down the block, and Owen, despite the feeling that his new friend might be crazy, hurried after him. Simon stepped onto the curb leading into the woods, and Owen, baffled at the sight (Simon's body seemed to be get-ting blurry now), ran to catch up.

Owen paused in confusion a few inches away. Simon, standing half in the woods and half out, grabbed his arm and tugged him up the curb. Owen gasped in amazement as the enormous forest suddenly became visible.

Together, the boys walked in: for the first time in history, two Outsiders entered Dunkerhook Woods.

CHAPTER 6

THE BROKEN CHAIN

As Simon and Owen were stepping into history, Ralfagon Wintrofline was sitting in a cramped room cluttered with piles of books, overflowing file cabinets, and scattered stacks of papers. This was his office at Milnes University. It wasn't always this messy; Eldonna straightened it up at least twice a week. When Ralfagon was lost in thought, however, he tended to invoke physics formulas without noticing. It was his version of thumb twiddling or pencil chewing, only his method caused small items to move around in random ways. It proved disastrous on the rare occasions he went into stores that sold glassware.

Ralfagon wasn't lost in thought now. He was hunched over the one clear spot on his desk, which was occupied by a thick blue Book. It was the Book of Physics, and it contained all the formulas, laws, and powers connected to the science of physics. Ralfagon never let the book out of his sight, and the cover kept it disguised from Outsiders; it read: *Teacher's Edition of Physics,* so any students or colleagues who happened to see it thought it was Professor Ralph Winter's ordinary teaching textbook.

Ralfagon's eyes were closed. If anybody walked into his office, they'd assume he'd fallen asleep and would wonder about the blue glow coming from the Book beneath his hands. Such an intrusion wasn't likely—the door to his office was closed and sealed with a force that few living beings on the planet (or off it) could break. And Ralfagon wasn't asleep; he was in a meeting.

"Now, Gilio, I thought we'd covered this: the problem is everyone's, and we must all do our part to help fix it." Ralfagon was using the Book to commune with the rest of the Council of Sciences: the Keepers of the various other Science Orders who were seated in their own private places, resting their hands on their own Books. "No, Allobero, there's no need to be so nasty to him." Ralfagon spoke aloud through force of habit, but it wasn't necessary; the Books linked the Keepers' minds. He listened quietly for a moment. "I agree with you on that, Gilio. I don't like the way that

Board member handled matters. It seems foolish to split up. I don't think it's paranoia; I, too, have felt something unusual and unpleasant brewing."

He listened for several moments, his mouth turning down at the corners. "Isn't there any way to change your minds? A way we could work together on this?" A long pause. "Very well. We'll resume talks in a month or two."

The blue glow cut off; Ralfagon's contact with the other Keepers was terminated. He sighed and rested his head on his hands, speaking directly to his Book. "That's it, I suppose; we're on our own. I only hope Gilio's wrong. If there is dark–ness brewing, it could mean the end of the entire Union. Maybe even the universe itself."

CHAPTER 7

That Fresh Vacuum Cleaner Scent

If you went back far enough through history, long before the invention of the chain saw, you'd find all of Lawnville and its neighboring towns covered in forest. The trees—then just average maples, elms, and oaks—had nothing better to do than shed their leaves every autumn and debate soil quality. Until centuries ago, when the Dutch settled the land. Many trees were chopped down, and the vast forest land was reduced to a relatively small patch of woods. Needless to say, the trees weren't too happy about this.

The Order of Physics, then led by Keeper Peteretep Van Silasalis, moved their base of operations from Amsterdam to the New World. Peteretep settled in the area that would one day be called Lawnville because, quite frankly, the grass really was greener there.

Peteretep chose a forest as a meeting place, since trees provided natural shelter from prying Outsider eyes. He chose those woods in particular for the same reason that, long before, the Druids had chosen to build Stonehenge on Salisbury Plain, England: the region naturally welcomed, even amplified, the use of powerful energies. In other words, it would be a good place from which to control the universe.

The Order worked hard, establishing long–lasting formulas to keep Outsiders from finding their woods. Soon the woods became completely isolated from non–Union members. Its hidden nature led the Order to name the woods *Dunkerhook*, meaning "dark corner" in Dutch; besides, the Order thought it sounded better than Treehenge.

Over time, Dunkerhook Woods soaked up much power from the formulas protecting it, as well as those practiced by the Order inside its borders. Every speck of dirt, every plant, and even the air became charged with qualities that made these woods unique among other forests. The trees, once ordinary, became sylvan behemoths. Although the woodland animals that lived there remained average in size and shape, they acquired a know–it–all demeanor that would seem downright snooty to animals dwelling in Outsider lands.

It's often debated if Dunkerhook Woods truly had a mind of its own, but at the very least, it had developed an attitude. It started generating the Breeze, using it to welcome the Order members whose presence had brought it such positive change. It apparently also developed the willpower to ignore the Order's protective formulas so it could extend its Breeze to whomever it wanted.

Thus, it used the Breeze to lure Simon to its border and invite him in. It allowed him to bring Owen along, and once inside, they felt the weight of Dunkerhook Woods. The Breeze embraced them, and every breath acted like a super-megadose of caffeine and sugar, only without the shakes or tooth decay.

The boys eagerly bounded down the path, marveling at the skyscraper-size forest. They veered off to explore, finding such wonders as a copse of bushes that grew naturally to resemble a pile of apples or a single tree with more trunks than a herd of elephants.

Finally, they reached the clearing, the focal point of all the Order's efforts, and stared at the ring of stumps.

"Hey, look at those!" Owen said. "How do you think that happened?"

"Looks like somebody made it," Simon said, "maybe for a meeting place."

Owen frowned. "Why would people meet in the middle of a forest?"

"People?" Simon said. "Maybe not. But aliens? Yeah. It could be where they shed their human disguises and make plans for world conquest."

Simon smiled and jumped onto Ralfagon's stump. "It's springy. Like a couch cushion! Owen, you've got to feel this!"

Owen shuddered. "What–if–it's–rotten–you–know–mushy–because–it's–filled–with–poison–or–something?"

Simon shook his head. "C'mon. I promise you, tree stumps don't bite."

If Simon knew more about the world, he might not have been so sure.

Owen walked over to a random stump and pushed down on it. "Spongy; cool."

Simon bounced some more. "Yup, just the way the aliens made 'em. No, not just aliens . . . alien wizards! Yeah, I'll bet this is where the most powerful alien wizard makes speeches from. And he waves his hands in the air while he casts his spells, wiggling his fingers." Simon did just that, unknowingly mimicking the gesture Ralfagon made while conducting the Order's ceremony.

Simon was about to learn an important lesson: never stand on an unusual tree stump and wiggle your fingers in the air in a place overflowing with such power and energy. In those types of places, anything could happen.

The Breeze suddenly whipped wildly around Simon. The air above his head shimmered, then glowed, and finally, it ripped.

The sound of air ripping is nothing like paper or fabric ripping. Try to imagine the noise of one hundred high-powered fans blowing at top speed. Add in the sound of several hundred pandas biting into several hundred stalks of bamboo while thousands of basketball fans stomp their feet, clap their hands, and cheer loudly. Toss in the *pop* of a single can of soda being opened, and the combined effect would not be that of air ripping. But it'd be close enough.

Simon was squinting at the glowing air when the rip happened. He gaped as a two-foot-diameter hole opened, revealing complete darkness inside, as if he was looking into a bottomless pit. For a split second, he smelled something musty and dry, like a rupturing vacuum cleaner bag filled to the brim with dust. He didn't recognize it, having never encountered the stink of time and space bending.

Simon was so surprised by the hole that he didn't have time to react as something fell from it. That something was a thick blue book—actually, a Book. The very same *Teacher's Edition* that belonged to Ralfagon Wintrofline, Keeper of the Order of Physics.

Two thuds followed: one from the Book conking Simon on the head and one from Simon plopping to the ground. (The Book hit the ground, too, but that sound was more of a *thunk*.)

As the two lay side by side on the path, the universe quietly trembled.

THE UNIVERSE WASN'T THE ONLY THING TREMBLING

There is nothing worse for a Narrator than the sound of space–time bending: it means the story's about to get confusing (what do you expect from things moving in time and space?). I watched in total disbelief as the Book of Physics appeared, and I almost fell off my chair when it hit Simon on the head.

What had happened? How could the Book, the *Teacher's Edition*, be there in Dunkerhook Woods when it had just been in Ralfagon's office? Backing up, why was that stupid forest letting those two boys see, much less enter it? And what would happen now that they had the Book to themselves? Surely they wouldn't be able to open and use it? No, that privilege was reserved for the Order of Physics' Keeper.

But what of that Keeper? Ralfagon *never* went anywhere without his Book; for it to appear on its own implied terrible things. Could this be related to Mermon Veenie and his mysterious hooded ally?

There were clearly dark things afoot, and it was up to me to understand them.

So I turned back to my Chronicle and took a sip of tea. Nobody should study the fate of the universe without a cup of tea in hand.

CHAPTER 8

A BOY AND HIS BOOK

I watched as Owen rushed to Simon's side. He'd seen movies and TV shows where doctors gave first aid, used electrical paddles, and even did mouth-to-mouth resuscitation. He shook his head. Nope, he wasn't going to do any of that.

Instead, he grabbed Simon's shoulder and shook him. "Hey! Simon, are you okay? Are you dead?" He shook him harder and, getting no response, panicked. "Come-on-don't-be-dead-this-is-no-fair-I-don't-know-what-to-do."

Finally, after racking his brain, Owen cocked his hand back and walloped Simon's cheek. Simon's eyes flew open, and he screamed.

"Owww! Owen, are you crazy?"

"Am–I–crazy–I–don't–know–you–tell–me–I–saw–a–book–come–out–of–nowhere–and–it–looked–like–it–killed–you–and–you–were–lying–there–so–what–am–I–supposed–to–do–it's–not–like–my–mom–lets–me–have–a–cell–phone–so–I–could–call–for–cops–or–an–ambulance–or–anything." He sucked in deeply, having exhausted his air supply.

All Simon could say to that was, "Oh." He saw Owen refueling for another blast of words and quickly held up his hands. "I'm okay, I think. My head hurts. And there's a big book that just popped out of nowhere." He sneezed, which only made his head hurt more. "Was someone vacuuming?" he asked, sniffing the air.

Owen didn't know how to answer that. "Can you sit up?" he asked. It was one of the shortest sentences he'd ever spoken.

Simon did. He winced as he touched the small bump the Book had left. Then he leaned toward the Book. Owen shrank back.

"Come on, Owen, it's just a book," Simon said.

Owen shook his head, his anxiety building. "It's not *just* anything. It–came–out–of–nowhere–and–attacked–don't–go–near–it!"

Simon ignored him and examined the Book. He read the plain white lettering: *Teacher's Edition of Physics*. There was nothing else on the cover except a thick, locked metal clasp keeping it tightly shut.

"What's physics?" Owen asked. Another short sentence; he was calming down.

"It's a type of science. Laws of the universe: light, heat, electricity. You know, like a rock falls when you drop it because of gravity. Stuff like that."

"Is it someone's schoolbook?" Owen asked.

Simon shook his head. "I don't know. It says *Teacher's Edition*; that's what teachers use. You know, with all the answers in it. Let's open it."

Simon reached for the Book but almost fell over.

Owen steadied him. "Simon, you don't look so good. You're pale and–maybe–you–have–a–concussion–and–you're–going to–pass–out. We should get you home."

Simon sorted out Owen's words. "Okay," he finally said. "But I'm taking this." He picked up the Book. "Wow . . . it's so light!"

(Indeed, although most of the Books were a foot tall, eight inches wide, and, in the case of physics, almost three inches thick, they each weighed the same as a medium–size paperback.)

Once Owen helped him to his feet, Simon put the Book into his backpack.

"You're taking it?" Owen asked. "It's–not–yours–it–came–out–of–nowhere–it–could–be–dangerous."

"It fell on me!" Simon exclaimed. "Finders keepers, right? Besides, it's just a book. How dangerous could it be?"

(If the universe had trembled before, it was probably snickering now.)

Owen made Simon walk slowly; it took them ten minutes to go a block and a half. Owen kept bringing up things he'd seen on medical shows. "Put some ice on your head and keep your feet elevated and drink plenty of fluids."

"Okay, I'll do all that; thanks, Owen. See you tomorrow in school."

"If you last that long! Be sure and tell your parents about your head so they know to call the doctor if you pass out or anything." Then Owen scampered off.

Inside his room, Simon put on a baseball cap to cover his bump and closed the blinds. He placed the Book on his desk and stared at it cautiously; it was probably magical. What did that mean? Was he stupid to touch it or, worse, to try to read it? "Probably," he whispered, "but I'm going to anyway."

Simon examined the metal clasp that kept the Book shut; there was no keyhole, and it looked sturdy enough to break a hammer. The second his fingers touched it, though, the clasp popped open.

A faint humming began; it sounded like it was coming from the Book. "Are you humming?" Simon whispered. The humming noise stopped, and Simon smiled nervously; either his imagination had just gotten stronger, or he was on the verge of something incredible. He held his breath as he opened the front cover, expecting all kinds of dangers or wonders.

Instead, he was faced with nothing but a column of crossed-out words. Only the last line was legible: it said *Ralfagon Wintrofline.*

Of course, the name Ralfagon Wintrofline wouldn't look too normal to anyone outside the Union. To Simon, it sounded like a type of bathroom cleaner or a brand of all-weather tire. But he somehow sensed that this was a name. In fact, the column reminded him of the list of names found on the inside covers of school library books. For one horrifying moment, Simon envisioned an alien librarian coming after him and demanding an extraterrestrial quarter as payment.

Simon wondered if he should add his name to the list. As if in response, a pen appeared, rising up out of the cover like it was surfacing from underwater. The words *Please sign in* appeared above the column in glowing blue ink. Simon's mouth dropped open, and without thinking, he grabbed the pen. It was clear, with blue ink inside that bubbled like a fresh glass of soda.

Why not? Simon thought. Numerous reasons, most of them involving extreme danger or deepening insanity, sprang to mind, but he ignored them. This was just too amazing to pass up.

He wrote his name beneath Ralfagon's, and the letters glowed brightly for a moment. The page now read *This Book is the property of Simon Bloom.* The words *Welcome, Keeper* appeared on the opposite page, and the humming started up again, even louder than before.

Simon returned the pen to the front cover and gasped when it melted back into the Book and vanished.

"And just what am I the Keeper of?" Simon whispered. He took a deep breath and turned the first page. And the next, and the one after.

Then he groaned.

It was a physics textbook. There was a title page, a table of contents, formulas, definitions, diagrams. It just looked like a more complicated version of the science books he read in school. He flipped to the chapter on gravity and groaned again. How, he wondered, could something magical be so boring?

He frowned at the thrumming Book. "Oh, be quiet."

The noise died away, but then bright blue words appeared. *Turn the page,* they said.

Simon did as he was told. He squinted, unsure of what he was looking at. There were several blue shapes and squiggles unlike anything he'd ever seen, but he somehow knew they meant something. As he stared, he felt something click in his brain, and though the symbols hadn't changed, they suddenly made sense to him. He realized that it was a language. A language that explained gravity.

Even Simon, with the little science he knew, could tell that the blue symbol language didn't quite match the regularly typed textbook material; there were some contradictions. It was, Simon thought, as if the usual textbook information only explained one part of things, but the language of blue shapes and squiggles had the full story. As he read on, he gasped. If he was reading it right, those symbols described how to *control* gravity!

Simon flipped back and forth between the pages and glanced over the laws of gravity. He already knew that on Earth, gravity pulled everything down toward the center of the planet (the reason why apples fall from trees or people fall when pushed off cliffs). Without it, everything would be weightless.

Simon looked at his picture of astronauts bouncing on the moon's surface. They could do so because the moon's gravity was one-sixth that of Earth. Then he flipped back to those squiggles in the Book. "Could *I* do that?" he wondered aloud. "Could I do *more* than that?"

As if in answer, the Book started its thrumming again. Simon realized there was only one way to find out. He cleared his throat, found the right symbols, and read them aloud. The words sounded like pure nonsense (even to me, and I'm the Narrator). It was that backward, forward, peanut buttery sound that, when I heard it, made me either want to clean my ears or get Simon a glass of milk.

The thrumming cut off abruptly. Simon looked around and frowned: there was no miraculous change in reality. He forced himself to laugh; it was his way of covering his disappointment. Then he realized his body did feel a little different, as if someone had just stopped pushing down on his shoulders.

Puzzled by this, Simon absently rubbed at the bump under his cap. The cap slid upward and he felt it pop off his head. He looked up in surprise as the cap floated away, turning end over end until it tapped the ceiling and gently bounced downward.

Startled, Simon flinched, and his left arm hit a cup on his desk. He groaned, expecting the soda inside to spill everywhere. Instead, the cup zipped away, smacked into the wall, and rebounded up. Most of the soda flowed out in a big blob as the cup spun toward the ceiling.

Simon leaned toward the amoebalike soda floating over his desk. He blew at it, making it quiver and break into globules that drifted off in different directions.

"No way!" Simon gasped. He stood up to get a closer look at the soda splotches, but instead of rising normally, he launched up from the chair. He instinctively swung out his arms, but before he could grab anything, his feet were off the floor and he was tumbling upward.

As he rose into the air, Simon realized what happened.

He had canceled gravity in his bedroom! He was floating!

CHAPTER 9

What Newton Said
(and Simon's Dirty Ceiling)

Simon drifted up and over the soda blobs, his arms and legs flailing wildly. For a moment, he was worried. Would this suddenly wear off and send him crashing to the floor? What if gravity never came back? What if the whole house was weightless? Or the whole world?

Then his back gently bumped the ceiling. Simon bobbed in the air and looked at his room below him. This was what he'd always dreamed about, but it wasn't his imagination. This was for real.

He let out a whoop, pushed his elbows against the ceiling, and somersaulted toward the floor. He laughed as he easily pushed off the wood floor with his hands, rebounding up like a giant basketball.

Simon streaked through the air and cheered, bouncing off the ceiling, the floor, and every wall. He spread his legs and arms differently with every leap to twist or spin in a new way. He counted how many flips he could do backward, forward, and sideways, loving every second. There was no fear of crashing or sense of falling because there was no up or down anymore. There wasn't even any dizziness. As far as Simon knew, there was no danger—just the joy of zero g.

"Now," he said, "let's see what else I can do with this Book." He aimed his bounces to take him back to the desk and grabbed at his chair to pull himself down. But the chair came off the ground and floated across the room; it was weightless, too. And that's when the trouble started.

See, while Simon knew the basics of gravity, he didn't know much more. For example, he didn't know the difference between mass and weight. Mass is the amount of solid, liquid, or gas that make up an object; the more mass something has, the more it weighs when gravity pulls on it. Size doesn't matter: a soccer ball and a bowling ball are about the same size, but the bowling ball is solid inside, weighs a lot more, and is *a lot* less fun to kick around.

Even when there's no gravity and no weight, things keep their mass. Remember that. It'll be important in a few seconds.

Another thing Simon should have learned before he started bouncing around his room was Isaac Newton's three laws of motion. But he was about to take a crash course. Literally.

The first is the law of inertia: a strange name for a simple idea. An unmoving object (like the chair) remains unmoving until an outside force (Simon pulling at it) affects it. Then it keeps moving (in this case, drifting across the room) until other forces (like gravity or air resistance or a collision with the wall) slow it down.

The second law builds on the first. It can be called the law of constant acceleration and says an object's speed depends on how much force is used on it. So the chair would only move as fast as Simon pulled it. The second law also says that because the chair has a lot of mass—more than the floating cup and cap—it takes more effort to move. Simon hadn't pulled it very hard, so the chair moved slowly.

The third law builds on the second and is sometimes called the law of conservation of momentum: a mouthful, I know. But that was the most important for Simon's zero-g adventures so far. It says every action has an equal and opposite reaction; it's why Simon floated into the air when he stood up. Each time he pushed against the ceiling, floor, or walls, he sent himself in the other direction. That was great for bounding around his room, yes, but it also meant that a light pull back on the chair equaled a light push forward on Simon.

Because Simon had more mass than the chair and he hadn't used much force on it, that light push forward didn't give him much speed. As Simon drifted near, he grabbed the window frame above his desk.

Unfortunately, Simon couldn't hold on to the frame; he floated back toward the center of the room. His missed grab had lost him a lot of momentum, and since he didn't push off the frame, Newton's second law made him slow down. A lot.

This was the zero-g equivalent of your car running out of gas or your legs getting too tired to push your skateboard, scooter, or unicycle (if you happen to like that type of ride). Simon drifted ever more slowly toward the center of his room, losing speed until he had practically stopped, bobbing several feet from anything: the walls, the ceiling, and the floor. Unlike anyone in a car or on a skateboard, scooter, or unicycle, Simon couldn't just walk away. He was stuck.

He tried swimming by scooping at the air with his arms and kicking with his legs. He pumped them hard, frantically trying to move. He switched from freestyle to breaststroke, sidestroke to backstroke, and even tried to dog-paddle. If he'd been underwater, he might have broken Olympic records. But because air was much thinner than water, he didn't move forward. Not an inch.

He wondered again, how long would this gravity-free thing last?

Then he heard something terrifying. "Simon?" His mom

was home! "What was all that noise a minute ago?" She'd heard him bouncing around his room!

He looked at the plastic cup, the soda globules, the baseball cap, and several toys—knocked loose by his bouncing—all floating around the room. What if she came in and saw them? Worse, what if she came in and noticed her son hovering in midair? She'd freak out!

He fought his rising panic; he had to calm down and find a way to keep her from coming upstairs. "Sorry, Mom," he yelled. "Dropped something."

"What are you doing?" Her voice was closer.

"Nothing!" Simon yelled louder. "Doing homework. Too busy to talk now!"

There was silence; had she stopped? Turned back? Or was she about to open the door? He looked up at the ceiling and let out a nervous breath. Then he gasped; had he drifted downward a tiny bit?

"Those didn't sound like homework noises!" his mom yelled. Simon heard a familiar creak; it was the loose step halfway up the stairs. She was coming; there was no time to lose!

Simon exhaled again, and as the air left his lips, he sank down a little farther. Yes! He was sure of it now: blowing air up sent him moving down. He blew as hard as he could, sinking a bit more.

He was still several feet from the ground so he kept at it, puffing so hard that his lungs started to hurt and his mouth went completely dry, but he was soon able to extend his fingers and just brush against the floor. He made himself wait until he could put both his palms against the floor. He knew he needed a hard push.

Finally, he was close enough; this was his chance! He shoved the floor, launching himself back up to the ceiling. He pushed off the ceiling with his legs, aiming for his desk. This time he grabbed the desk itself, pulling on the edge to keep from slipping away again. Fortunately for Simon, the desk had too much mass for him to move it like he had the chair.

Carefully, oh, so carefully, he pulled himself down until he was face-to-Book with the open *Teacher's Edition*. His whole body was stretched out up and behind him, dangling as if held up by invisible wires. He scanned the pages for the way to undo the gravity problem.

"Simon? Open this door!" There was a loud knocking; she was right outside!

"How do I bring the stupid gravity back?" he muttered. The symbols he read before glowed in reverse order, from the last one to the first. Was the Book telling him how to make things normal again?

Seeing no other choice, he read the symbols in reverse and instantly came crashing down to the floor. So did the chair, the hat, the toys, the cup, and the soda, which splashed all over.

With that, his mom burst through the door. "What was

that noise?" She stared at the sight of her son sprawled on the floor in front of his desk, his hands gripping the edge of it. His desk chair was near the door.

Simon groaned and grabbed his baseball cap. He popped it back on his head to cover the bump and then tugged himself to his feet.

"Sorry, Mom. I, uh, was doing some homework and spilled some soda; then I slipped and fell." He coughed nervously. "And knocked the chair over."

Sylvia glanced at the mess and then raised an eyebrow at the huge Book. "What is that enormous thing on your desk?"

Simon struggled to remain calm. "That? Just a science book."

Sylvia brightened instantly. "Wonderful! Pizza okay for dinner?" Without waiting for an answer, she said, "It'll be here in thirty minutes or less. Clean this mess up, then come on down." She left and shut the door.

Simon sighed with relief. Then he glanced upward and groaned. Now he had to find a way to get his footprints off the ceiling.

CHAPTER 10

LICENSE TO FLY

The next morning, Simon ran down the stairs for breakfast. He was exhausted from practicing the gravity formula late into the night, but he was too excited to care. He had powers that no other eleven-year-old did, and he didn't have to come from another planet, get bitten by a spider, or be bombarded by radiation to get them.

Plus, he wasn't too worried about his weariness. The Book warned him, through the printed blue messages, that heavy use of the formulas would tire him for at least the first week or two. It also told him that sleep and food would help him recover.

He got to the table and, as usual, found his parents looking over paperwork as they ate. Simon looked at his mom, polished and professional in her business attire. Then he looked at his dad, shirt misbuttoned and hair frizzy like a mad scientist who'd been electrocuted.

Sylvia and Steven Bloom were utterly wrapped up in their worlds, but last night proved that there was a small danger of them finding out about his Book. He knew his mother wouldn't be able to handle the news, and his father would probably drag him into the lab for testing. Simon frowned; he'd have to be very careful with his secret.

Neither parent looked up as Simon sat down. "Did you finish your schoolwork?" Sylvia asked, making a notation on a memo.

"Yes," Simon said, suddenly nervous that she'd ask him about it.

"That's my go-getter," Sylvia said at the same time that Steven said, "Good job, pal." They glanced up at him, smiled, and went back to their papers.

So Simon ate his breakfast (actually, he ate two break-fasts' worth in order to get his strength back) and said good-bye. He stepped outside, with the Book tucked away at the bottom of his backpack, and he thought about using the gravity formula to get to school. If he was careful, he could probably do it without being seen.

Then something caught his eye in the maple tree on his front lawn.

There, on one long, bare branch jutting past the leaves,

sat a tiny bird—a sparrow—with gray-brown plumage and a horizontal white stripe across its belly.

Most kids would have paid no mind to the bird, but Simon was not most kids. He watched it carefully; something wasn't right. Sure, it looked ordinary enough. But it wasn't chirping, it wasn't hanging around with other birds, and it wasn't moving. At all. It was staring. Yes, the more Simon thought about it, this sparrow was *definitely* checking him out.

"What are you looking at?" Simon asked aloud.

The bird suddenly turned its head away and didn't look at Simon again. It looked everywhere else but at him, which made it all the more obvious to Simon that it *had* been watching him. That bird was a spy.

I may be crazy or just overtired, Simon thought, *but if that bird is spying on me, I don't want to use my gravity control.* There could be other spies, maybe wearing a clever disguise. A tree that's really hiding a teacher. A mailbox with a policeman peeking out. A large dog that's really a government official looking to quarantine him for study and use as the next superweapon. There were too many risks, so Simon just walked to school.

From time to time, he peeked over his shoulder while pretending to tie his shoe, check his watch, or just stretch and yawn. Each time, he spotted that same sparrow (the stripe on its belly was a dead giveaway). Every time Simon looked, the bird started that moving-its-head-around routine again, trying to look innocent.

Once at school, Simon was safe; no birds allowed. He didn't even sit near a window in any of his classes. He spent the entire day trying to avoid everyone even more than usual; he even stayed inside at lunchtime.

By his last class, Simon wondered if he'd just been paranoid about the bird. The only strange thing at school was Alysha at the lockers that morning. "You look different," she said with a puzzled glance. "Taller, maybe."

(In fact, Simon *had* grown an eighth of an inch overnight, but Alysha was actually noticing the residue left by the energies of Dunkerhook Woods. They were known to give visitors an invisible glow and an untouchable warmth that made their teeth brighter, hair shinier, and earwax less gooshy.)

Before Simon could think of a response, Marcus stopped by. Simon used the distraction to slip away.

Mostly, Simon just waited and waited, eager for the day to end. The bells had never been more grating or the hallway chatter more jarring . . . even the click of the classroom clock pained him. At last school let out, and Simon and Owen met up by the playground exit of the school. Owen asked where Simon had been during lunch, but Simon, deciding his bird–spy fear was too weird to bring up, just shrugged.

As they walked away from school together, Simon listened to Owen talk about the day in his normal, superfast style. Simon listened as best as he could; he was still fighting his tiredness and looking around for the bird.

Finally, as they stepped onto Jerome Street, Simon couldn't hold back any longer. He interrupted Owen (who was describing the dangers of plastic forks at lunchtime). "Owen, you are not going to believe this. I barely believe it and I lived it. But that Book that fell on my head is magical! Supermagical! But real! I can't wait to show you; you're going to love it!"

Owen, already anxious about the forks, sputtered, "What do you mean, 'magical'?"

"You'll see," Simon said. They turned down Van Silas, and the Breeze blew over Simon, making him feel recharged.

As on the day before, Owen claimed he couldn't see the woods until they were stepping up onto the trail. Once inside, though, he smiled at the Breeze's revitalizing touch and marveled at the woods. "Come on, Simon, tell me what you found out about the Book. Do you know where it came from or what it does?"

Simon pulled the Book out of his backpack and showed it to Owen. "Check it out." He opened it and showed his friend his name beneath Ralfagon's.

"Oh. Cool," Owen said.

Simon could tell he wasn't impressed, so he told Owen about his activities the night before. He was disappointed by Owen's reaction: he just shrugged. "I guess that's cool," he said.

"Are you crazy? Did you hear me? I can control gravity, Owen! What, you don't believe me?"

Owen didn't say a word, but he looked away guiltily.

"Okay," Simon said. "Just watch." He held the Book in his hands, wanting to hang on to it just in case things got tricky again. Then he looked up and noticed a problem: there was no ceiling. The last thing he wanted to do was to keep floating up into space; that would be dangerous with or without the Book.

Instead, he studied the Book again, deciding exactly which symbols would do what he wanted. All he had to do was arrange them into the right formula. "Okay, here we go. Something a little different from what I did last night." He gestured from their bodies to the ground. "This is known as one g: normal Earth gravity. Jump up in the air as high as you can."

Owen gave Simon a doubtful look and jumped; his short legs gave him maybe four inches of lift.

Simon whistled. "Wow. Impressive. Now, watch me." He spoke the formula in that indecipherable Book language. Owen stared at him as if he'd come from another planet.

"This is one-fiftieth g," Simon said. "You might want to stand back." Then Simon tucked the Book under his arm and jumped as hard as he could.

Owen gaped as Simon launched up into the air, yelling, "Yeeeee-haa!" His hair blew back and his windbreaker flapped around him as he hurtled almost fifty feet into the air. It was easy; he now weighed one-fiftieth of his normal weight, but his leg muscles still delivered the normal amount of force.

Coming down was scarier: he was fifty feet above the ground, after all. Fortunately for Simon, less gravity also meant a slower fall. Rather than plummet down, he gracefully descended and landed on his feet a little farther down the path.

Owen stared for a second before running to Simon. "How did you do that?"

Simon laughed. "With this Book, I think I can do anything!"

Owen looked horrified. "What do you mean, 'anything'?"

Simon thought about the symbols for gravity. Now that he understood this language, he could command gravity and actually observe how he'd changed things. He looked around him, focusing not on what he saw with his eyes but on what he could feel.

It was like he'd gained a sixth sense. Gravity was more complicated than he ever thought: it connected everything around him like an enormous, intricate web. Every twist, curve, and pocket in the web affected the way the universe worked. And he could change those twists, curves, and pockets.

"With this Book," Simon said, "I can control all of physics. Gravity is just the beginning." He struggled not to laugh at the look Owen gave him. It was probably the face a rabbit made before it dug a hole to hide in.

"Are-you-crazy-did-you-see-how-high-you-went-you-could-get-yourself-killed!" Owen shouted.

"Owen, it's completely safe. I swear. C'mon, you try."

Owen backed away, his hands up, as if to ward off all the tacos and shredded lettuce in the world. (His was a strange phobia, but a phobia nonetheless.)

Simon sighed. He'd have to prove to Owen just how much fun this was. He made a new formula, changing his gravity to one-five-hundredth g.

"Just watch me again and you'll see how easy it is," Simon said. Once again, he jumped up as hard as he could; this time, his jump sent him hurtling about five hundred feet in the air!

Just think about it: the biggest, redwood-size trees in Dunkerhook Woods are about two hundred feet tall. The Statue of Liberty is about three hundred feet tall. The Great Pyramid of Giza in Egypt is four hundred and eighty-one feet high. And Simon jumped higher than all of those.

His leap carried him far above the trees, and for a few seconds, he was able to see the tops of houses, the top of his school, the top of the huge town water tower. He could see all of Lawnville—in fact, several neighboring towns—spread out around him. He didn't have much time to enjoy it, though.

Simon yelped as a gust of wind hit him. This wasn't the gentle, energizing Breeze; he was too far above Dunkerhook Woods for that. No, this was real wind, the kind of gust that sends kites soaring hopelessly out of control and balloons far beyond their owners' grasp.

At one–five–hundredth g, Simon weighed about the same as two candy bars—fortunately, more than a balloon or a kite. Also, his mass hadn't changed, so he wouldn't be blown away too swiftly. Still, the wind was strong enough to move him; instead of gently descending back down to where Owen waited, he drifted away.

Simon's first reaction was panic. What if he landed in the middle of a highway and got smashed by a car? Or what if he got hit by a passing airplane? Or, worst of all, what if the wind blew him so hard that he never landed at all?

"Keep calm!" he hissed to himself. "What'd I do last night?" After dinner, he'd practiced increasing his weight gradually so he could sink gently to the ground. This would work now, too. But he had to be careful. Too much gravity would send him crashing down to the ground in a messy, painful way.

Simon worked cautiously, using the formula words like a gravity–controlling dimmer switch. He was able to add ounces instead of pounds, and soon the wind wasn't moving him anymore; he was making his way down.

The damage had been done, though. He was no longer heading toward the dirt path. As he dropped lower and lower, he saw he was going to land on a thin branch near the top of one of the tallest trees in Dunkerhook Woods.

Simon clutched the Book in one hand and wrapped his

arms around the branch with the other. He felt the branch creak dangerously; he quickly adjusted his gravity formula, making him lighter again. Too much weight and he'd go crashing through all the branches, two hundred feet straight down. Ouch.

What next? He couldn't hop down from branch to branch—what if a branch broke? Or what if he hit his head and knocked himself out?

Simon thought back to the night before. Direction hadn't mattered when he was bouncing around his room, so it shouldn't matter here either. The path and the forest floor didn't have to be down; for him, down was wherever he commanded it to be. He changed the words of his formula and watched gravity around him twist in response. For everything else in the forest, all was normal, but for Simon, gravity now pulled him toward the tree trunk instead of the ground. Now the tree trunk *was* his ground!

Simon stood up straight and started walking down the tree, as if it were a narrow walkway. He steadied himself with the branches as he went, using them to cut down on how much he bounced; just like the astronauts on the moon, his reduced gravity could have sent him flying off with a misstep. He increased his weight little by little as the trunk got thicker and sturdier.

At last, Simon got close to the bottom of the tree; the forest floor was a huge dirt wall to him. Now he had to find a way to switch gravity back without smacking face-first into the dirt.

As he stood there, Simon heard Owen calling for him. Simon yelled back, and after some back and forth, Owen came panting over to him.

"You're-alive-I-can't-believe-it-you-just-disappeared-you-went-so-high-I-thought-you-went-up-into-space!" Owen craned his head back to look Simon in the face. "Why are you standing like that on the tree trunk?"

Simon took a deep breath to stay calm. This was just like his *Relativity* poster, with him at a right angle to Owen. It was a lot scarier than he'd guessed.

Finally, Simon gulped and jumped off the tree trunk, simultaneously changing his personal gravity to match Owen's. He twisted in midair, landing on his feet, but then he stumbled to the forest floor.

Simon lay flat for a few minutes, hugging the dirt. It was good to be on the ground again. "Maybe," he said haltingly, "maybe we should stop. For today." By the time he got to his knees and looked up, he saw Owen was already ten feet down the path, heading toward Van Silas Way.

Simon hurried to catch up. "Guess you're not going to argue over that."

THIS KEEPER IS A KEEPER

I was impressed by what Simon had accomplished. First, he was somehow chosen to receive one of the greatest honors in the known galaxy, becoming a Keeper, while skipping the hurdles that others had to endure (such as rigorous testing, special training, and various eating contests). Second, he was the youngest Keeper ever (and the shortest, though Gilio Skidowsa of Biology ran a close second). Third, he was coming up with remarkably innovative ways of using his power.

From the time Simon got home that Tuesday to the time he left for school the next day, almost all he did was eat and sleep to counter the tiredness from his gravity use. He was scared to go back to jumping with gravity right away, but he still dragged Owen back to the woods and insisted on practicing other uses of the power. By the end of their session in the woods on Wednesday, he had regained much of his confidence with that law of physics. That's probably what led to his next mistake.

CHAPTER 11

FOLLOWING THE TRAIL

It was lunchtime on Thursday afternoon, and Alysha Davis was headed to her locker, where she'd forgotten the sandwich her father had packed that morning. As she walked down the empty halls, she sighed. "Guess I spaced out," she said to herself. "I'm turning into Simon Bloom." She chuckled.

As she turned the corner, Alysha froze. There, at the far end of the hall, was Simon himself. She watched in awe as Simon balanced a huge stack of books on the tip of one finger!

Alysha squinted to be sure she was seeing right. Sure enough, they were all on one finger, yet he was holding them as easily as a stack of crackers! Then Alysha's jaw dropped as Simon tossed the books in the air and caught them on the tip of his other finger, as if they weighed almost nothing. The top book wobbled and dropped, but before it hit the ground, Simon kicked it back up with his foot like a Hacky Sack.

Alysha couldn't keep from gasping loudly.

Simon whipped his head around, and they locked eyes. He quickly put both hands under the stack, whispered something, and dropped the books all around him. He made a show of looking embarrassed. "Whoops. Those were heavy!"

Alysha stood and gaped; she was unable to move or say anything more as Simon tossed his books back into his locker and dashed out the far exit to the playground. By the time she went after him, he was out of sight.

Alysha couldn't get that image out of her mind for the rest of the day, but every time she tried to talk to Simon, he hurried off. Finally, after their last class—gym—she cornered him at their lockers. Coming up behind him as he stuffed books into his bag, she cleared her throat.

"Okay, what's going on with you?" Alysha demanded.

"What do you mean?"

She folded her arms and tapped one foot. "Back when we used to hang out, you always came up with those goofy ideas and funny stories. That was great. Then you started daydreaming all the time; fine, that's your deal. You zone out through classes and lunch; whatever, it's your life. But this week . . . something's different. You've been getting this weird smile at the end of the day, just before you meet up with that short kid. What's his name . . ."

"Owen?"

"Right." She leaned in. "Then you balance all those books on one finger?"

"W–what are you talking about?" Simon stammered.

Alysha rolled her eyes. "Please. Do *not* play dumb with me, Simon Bloom. I've known you for too long. I saw it all. First the balancing, then the kick. How did you do that?"

"You mean when you were standing all the way over there at the end of the hall?" Simon asked. "In this dim hall-way light? Maybe it's time for glasses, huh?"

"That's your answer?" Alysha demanded. "Get glasses?"

"There's always contact lenses. But you made a mistake, and I have to run!" Simon closed his backpack and ran off.

Alysha stared after him and frowned. She *had* to know what he was up to!

On Friday morning, Alysha's mind was a jumble as her father drove her to school. When they arrived, she gave him a kiss and paused as she opened the door. She'd made a decision. "Dad, I'm going to be home late today."

"Sure, honey, just be back by dinnertime," her father replied before driving off.

Alysha smiled as she walked across the front lawn of the school; kids were everywhere, playing Hacky Sack or Frisbee, rushing to finish homework, or just standing around and chatting. Her mind was still elsewhere as she headed toward her friends, gathered around the concrete steps at the school's front entrance.

Tall, blond Rachelle James came over to her, stepping away from the group. "Allie, what's with the outfit?"

Alysha looked down and saw she was wearing jeans, a sleeveless sweater, and a comfy pair of sneakers. It was fine for most kids at school, but Alysha's crowd, especially Rachelle, always dressed to impress. Alysha, feeling distracted, had thrown on lazy Sunday afternoon clothes.

Alysha faked a frown. "Bad laundry day."

Rachelle swept back her hair and groaned theatrically. "Ugh! You must be ready to *kill* your parents."

"Yeah," Alysha said. Actually, she liked not worrying about her clothes for once.

She looked past Rachelle and saw Marcus gazing at her. Rachelle followed her eyes. "Doesn't he look cute today? He'll be at Nezzo's after school."

Nezzo's, the best pizzeria in Lawnville, was a short walk from Martin Van Buren Elementary. Rachelle and her pack of girls always went there after school when Marcus and the boys went, and as the cool kids of the sixth grade, they always took the two big tables in the front of the restaurant. Since older kids usually went to places closer to the junior high and high schools, Marcus and the others had their run of the place. Marcus called their territory the Turf Tables, and he was ruthless to anyone not in their group who tried to sit there.

Alysha used to think sitting with Rachelle and the others at the Turf Tables was such a big deal, but today she had other things on her mind.

"Allie? Did you hear me?"

Alysha blinked. "Huh? Sorry, zoned out there."

"I was making sure you were coming with us to Nezzo's after school."

"Oh, I don't think I can," Alysha said. She faked a sad face. "My parents want me home right after school today."

Rachelle gave her a sympathetic look. "First they mess up your outfits, and then they sabotage your social life."

"Yeah, too bad," Alysha replied. "Hey, I've got to get inside. See you later." Alysha waved to the group, trying to ignore Marcus's wide smile; he looked like a hungry shark.

She strode down the hall thinking about why she'd lied to Rachelle about Nezzo's: the same reason she'd told her dad she'd be home late. Simon Bloom.

It wasn't just what he'd done with the books, although she was burning to know more about that. She liked that he didn't care about fashion or popularity. She liked that he had all those wacky ideas. And maybe she missed being his friend.

As Alysha watched Simon come into class in his usual distracted way, a dry, English-accented voice rang out from the hall. "A word with you, Mr. Bloom?"

Simon stepped outside the classroom door, and Alysha couldn't resist the chance to eavesdrop. She snapped the point off her pencil and went to the pencil sharpener near the door. She leaned as close to the doorway as she could and strained to hear Miss Fanstrom's voice.

"Mr. Bloom, I've become curious about you once again. I hope you don't mind my scrutiny; that means attention, by the way. No? Good. I see that the bump on your head is healing nicely. Oh, don't look so shocked, Mr. Bloom. Just because your parents are lost in their worlds doesn't mean every adult is. An important lesson, that. Your actions, no matter how well hidden, might not go unnoticed by others. Some of this scrutiny may be welcome but some is most unwelcome. Do you follow me?"

Alysha leaned closer to the doorway as Simon said, "No, Miss Fanstrom."

"Be aware that others might take notice as you go about your business. Be careful. And be ready for trouble if you should find it. Or if it should find you."

Alysha risked looking around the door frame. Miss Fanstrom was standing straight, briefcase in hand, facing Simon. Then Alysha stifled a gasp. The top of Miss Fanstrom's bizarre hair was bent over, and it looked like it was pointing right at her.

Alysha jumped back out of the doorway and quickly sharpened her pencil. She turned back to the classroom and saw Marcus Van Ny staring right at her. Had he seen her spying on Simon?

At lunchtime, Alysha looked out at the playground and

saw Simon and Owen sitting atop a concrete tube, ignoring the younger kids running and screaming around them. Simon was pointing at something in a tree just outside the playground. Squinting, Alysha thought she saw a small bird fly away.

What was Miss Fanstrom talking about? Alysha wondered. Where did Simon and Owen go after school every day? Was Owen a part of Simon's secret?

Later in class, Alysha was startled as a neatly folded note landed on her desk. She saw Rachelle smiling at her. Alysha opened it and read: *Marcus wants you to sit next to him at TT! You've got to come to Nezzo's!*

Alysha fought back a shudder at the thought of Marcus sitting shoulder to shoulder with her at those obnoxious Turf Tables. She faked a frown as she met Rachelle's eyes. She wrote, *Want to but can't. Sorry.* ☹, folded the note back up, and tossed it to Rachelle.

When class let out, she rushed to her locker to get her books. She had to hurry if her plan was going to work.

She hid in the playground and watched Simon and Owen walk out of the school. When they were far enough ahead, she followed.

Alysha couldn't hear them, but she could tell Owen was rattling on about something. She didn't know him well, but she knew how twitchy he was. Simon was nodding as he walked, occasionally glancing at the trees along the street.

Alysha watched the two boys walk toward the dead end on Van Silas Way. And then they disappeared.

Alysha blinked in confusion. Something in her brain told her there was nothing to worry about, nothing to think about on Van Silas Way; she must have been mistaken about where Simon and Owen were headed.

She was about to turn and leave when she felt the tiniest hint of the Breeze. Not even a touch or caress—more of a tickle. It was just enough to make her continue down the street, heading for the dead end. She saw nothing unusual, but she kept on walking to feel more of that amazing Breeze . . . and then she tripped over something and fell forward onto her hands and knees.

Alysha looked up from the ground and gasped. Instead of being on the asphalt street, she was on a dirt path in the midst of a forest she'd never noticed before. It had monstrous trees that stretched high into the sky, dwarfing the houses on either side. And ahead of her, farther down the trail, were Simon and Owen.

Alysha hurried after them, moving quietly along the path in these mysterious woods.

CHAPTER 12

THE DIRT CAPADES

Simon and Owen headed toward the clearing. "C'mon, you've got to try this," Simon said.

Owen shook his head.

"I swear I'll be careful! I've really got the hang of gravity now; I can do something simple but fun."

Owen just shook his head again.

Simon picked up three fist-size rocks from the forest floor and started to juggle them. Then he spoke his formula, reducing their gravity so they fell more slowly. He quickly grabbed more rocks and used his gravity control on them, too; within seconds, he was juggling ten rocks at once.

Owen stared. "Cool! I didn't know you could juggle!"

"There are lots of things you don't know I can do," Simon said. "But if you think this is something, wait'll you let me try a formula on you."

"I knew it!" a girl's voice interrupted. "You *are* up to something!"

Simon and Owen turned pale as Alysha Davis stomped down the path toward them. Simon forgot to catch the rocks, and all ten drifted down to the dirt.

Alysha stared openmouthed. Before Simon or Owen could react, she dove forward and picked up one rock. She hefted it in her hand, confirming what her eyes had told her. Then she looked up at Simon. "How?" she asked.

Owen's mouth moved up and down, but no words came out.

"What are you doing here?" Simon recovered enough to ask.

Alysha crossed her arms over her chest. "I want to know how you did this. And that thing with your books yesterday."

Owen took a step back from her, his mouth still flapping uselessly.

Simon frowned. "You shouldn't be here. How did you get into the woods?"

"You didn't answer my question."

"You didn't answer mine."

Alysha rolled her eyes. "I asked you first. But if you want to be a baby, fine. It's a free country. What's the big deal?"

"The big deal is . . ." Simon paused; he didn't know what to say.

To his amazement, Owen did. "The–big–deal–is–that–this–is–our–place–not–yours. Why–can't–you–let–us–have–one–place–where–we–don't–have–to–get–picked–on?"

Alysha held up her hands. "Whoa, boy, relax. Breathe. You're like that cartoon mouse."

"Mickey?" Simon asked.

"She means Speedy Gonzales, and no, I'm not . . . I just . . ." Owen took a breath and continued. "My mouth can't keep up with what I want to say sometimes." He paused for a moment. "I can speak normally if I want to, but that's not the point." He paused again. "The point is, this is *our* private place."

"What, are you scared of me or something?" Alysha asked.

"Not you," Owen said. "But you'll bring your friends, and soon Marcus and Barry and those guys will come here, too, and then me and Simon won't have anyplace to go that'll be safe, and that's not fair!"

Alysha and Simon both stood silently, sorting out what Owen had said. "I won't tell anyone anything," Alysha said. "Especially not Marcus. It's not their business." She held up her hands, palms out. "*I'm* not mean to you; I just hang out with some people who are. There's a difference, you know."

Simon frowned. "Not a big difference."

"I guess you're right," Alysha said, her voice barely above a whisper.

Simon sighed. "You swear you don't want to bring Marcus or any of that group in here?"

Alysha shook her head. "I can do stuff without them, you know. Besides, it's just a forest."

"*Just* a forest?" Simon said. "Are you nuts? Have you *ever* seen it before?"

Alysha chewed her bottom lip. "Okay, so that was weird. One minute, you guys had disappeared down a dead-end street, and the next . . . the next, I was in a forest." She gazed up at the towering trees. "I guess I just never noticed it before."

"It's hidden. Wait, how did you get in? Owen *never* notices it until I bring him in."

Alysha told them about that hint of wind she'd felt and how she'd tripped.

Simon looked around, breathing in the energy-filled air of the woods. "Wind? That Breeze. It *must* be that. That's what called me here, and that's what let you in, too. The Breeze must be part of the place's magic."

Alysha pounced. "Magic? What?"

"It's the place," Simon said. "It's special somehow. Can't you feel it?"

Alysha took a step back. "I don't know. Maybe."

Simon made up his mind. "Okay. Here's the truth." He gestured with his backpack. "I found a Book that lets me control the laws of physics."

Alysha stared at him for a minute, glanced over at Owen (who looked away), then rolled her eyes. "Yeah, right."

"It's true!" Owen shouted. "I've seen it!"

"Simon, your games were fun when we were seven, but that's old now."

"Do you want me to prove it?" Simon asked.

"Okay, show me what you got," she said.

Simon nodded. "I looked up a new formula: friction. It's the resistance between two objects when they rub against each other. It's what makes things stick together, and without it, things are all slippery. So there's a lot of friction when you rub against sandpaper but very little when you slide along a freshly waxed floor."

Alysha faked a yawn. "Okay, so let's go, Merlin. Dazzle me."

Simon pulled out the Book and opened it. He said, "Friction," and smiled proudly at Alysha and Owen as the pages flipped right to the section on friction.

Alysha folded her arms. "Nice gimmick."

"You're not a very open-minded person, are you?" Simon asked.

"I promise I won't tell anyone else about this, fine," Alysha said. "But if you want me to believe you can do magic, I'll need to see real proof. To do otherwise"—she looked at Owen—"would be ignorant."

"It's not really magic, I don't think," Simon said. "It's science. This Book tells me how science really works, and I can command it. It only *looks* like magic if you don't understand." Seeing her doubt, he nodded. "Just wait."

"Good, show her what you can do!" Owen said. "You did read carefully and practice, right?" he asked quietly.

"Yeah, yeah, sure," Simon said. "Don't worry." He glanced at Alysha. "These symbols are like a language. I just have to make sure I'm saying the right thing." He spoke a handful of nonsensical words. "Done."

Alysha looked around. "Sorry, Science Boy. Nothing's changed."

"Oh no?" Simon said. "Walk that way." He pointed toward the clearing.

Alysha took one step, and her feet slid out from under her as if she'd stepped on the biggest, slipperiest banana peel ever made. She fell on her butt and started sliding forward along the dirt path.

She let out a piercing scream. "Siiiiiiimmmoooooonnn! What did you do?"

"I took away your body's kinetic friction," Simon yelled. "Believe me now?"

She was speeding down the trail, her hands clawing uselessly at the dirt. Without any friction, everything was slicker than even the smoothest ice. "Yes! Now make it stop!"

Simon smiled wickedly. "I've got a better idea. Oh, Owen?"

Owen was looking at Alysha with a triumphant smile on his face; he turned to Simon and his eyes widened. He only had time to say, "No, wait—"

Simon directed the formula at Owen, who was already

starting to move away. As the formula kicked in, he slipped forward, fell onto his stomach, and started belly-sliding in the same direction as Alysha.

"I'm coming, too!" Simon yelled. He used the formula on himself but gave his toes a bit of friction so he could use his feet to push off and pick up speed. While Alysha and Owen were slipping, he could actually dirt-skate. "Yeaahhh! Just like ice-skating!" he yelled.

Simon zoomed after Owen and Alysha as they slid toward the clearing. Owen was moaning loudly, while Alysha was now shouting with delight.

"This is awesome!" she cheered. "Way better than skating!" She streaked along effortlessly, laughing as she zoomed through the clearing. Fortunately, there were no tree stumps in her way.

Owen whimpered as he sped headfirst. He was like a puck whizzing along the ice in a hockey game, only there was no net to catch him.

Simon pumped his feet, speeding forward so he could catch up to Owen. He looked down and waved. "So what do you think?"

"Please-please-please-make-me-stop!"

Alysha's scream yanked Simon's attention away. "Simon! Help!" She was past the clearing. Up ahead was the ravine that had formed during the Order's meeting . . . and Alysha was seconds away from going over the edge.

CHAPTER 13

GRAVITY IS FOR SUCKERS

"Don't worry, Owen," Simon shouted, "I'll figure this out before you get there." He sprint-skated toward Alysha, the trees blurring as he rushed by. He was starting to get winded; even without friction, it was tiring to run that hard.

Simon passed Alysha. "I'll save you, just hold on!" he yelled.

"Hold on to what?" Alysha yelled back.

Although the woods, as Ralfagon had predicted, was slowly fixing the gap on its own, the space was still close to thirty feet across. Simon would have to reverse the friction formula and fast.

In his hurry, Simon bobbled the Book. Since he had canceled friction while holding it, it was as friction-free as he was. It wasn't slippery to him, but it kept going when it hit the ground, sliding at matching speed. He couldn't bend over to grab it without falling, and he couldn't remember the formula's language to stop.

"Simon! Turn it off!" Alysha screamed from dozens of feet behind him.

Simon groaned. "Stupid, stupid, what are those words?" He was nearing the edge of the ravine. It was about twenty feet deep, and he had no doubt that falling down it would either kill them or at least hurt a whole lot.

He got an idea. It was going to take excellent timing: he'd only have one chance. He sprint-skated even faster so he was ahead of the Book when he reached the gap. Then he spoke his gravity formula.

"Simon, no!" Alysha cried out, but she was too late. Simon sailed over the edge of the gap. Only he didn't fall.

Simon had canceled the gravity right over the gap; instead of falling, he launched across it. He spun in midair so his hands were where his feet should have been, and he managed to grab the Book as it went over the edge.

His momentum kept him going; he spun as he soared, weightless, through the air. But Simon knew that Alysha and Owen weren't used to moving in zero g; they could collide with each other or drift back into the regular gravity zone and fall. He held the Book tightly. "Show me the friction-reversal formula!" he said.

The Book opened to the right page, to the exact words Simon needed to fix things. Simon twisted in midair and saw Alysha coming up to the edge. He waited for the precise moment and multiplied her friction to fifty times more than normal so her momentum wouldn't carry her into the chasm.

Alysha was jolted to a halt with only her rear end still on the ground. She was literally hanging on to the edge by the seat of her pants.

Simon continued spinning through the air to the other side of the gap. He used his gravity formula to make him light enough to land gently and then used friction to stop. He turned and saw Owen going over headfirst. Simon increased Owen's friction just in time, so the tips of his sneakers gripped the edge.

Simon burst into laughter. The no-gravity zone over the chasm kept Alysha's legs and Owen's body floating above it. Owen was flapping like a towel on a clothesline.

Alysha whooped. "That was . . . wow! I mean, wow."

Owen struggled to keep his voice steady as his body billowed. "Simon. Bloom. Let. Me. Down." This only made Alysha and Simon laugh harder.

Alysha clapped and cheered. "Okay, okay, you win. Magic, science, whatever you want to call it—I've never seen anything like it!"

Owen twisted his head around to glare at her, speaking remarkably slowly. "Yeah? No kidding."

"I'll be right there," Simon called out. He wasn't eager to take another low-gravity jump right then, so instead he changed his friction so his hands and feet would stick and unstick to the chasm wall. He climbed down and then up the other side, like Spider-Man.

Once he was back on the path, Simon dragged Alysha and Owen back from the edge of the gap and returned all gravity and friction to normal.

Owen scrunched his face up into a furious snarl.

"Sorry, Owen," Simon said, "but you've got to admit it was a little fun, right?"

Owen glared at him and smacked away the bits of dirt that had stuck to him while floating over the gap. "I want to go home."

"Come on," Simon said, "when you were sliding . . . I saw you smile."

Owen grumbled. "That was the wind pushing my lips back."

"Owen, please!" Alysha said. "That was amazing! It was ten times better than any roller coaster!"

Owen frowned. "Don't like roller coasters."

"You honestly hated it?" Simon asked.

Owen tried to hold a glare, but a bit of a smile peeked out. "I guess it was kind of cool." He paused. "But did you have to make me slide on my stomach like that? *She* got to sit down!"

Alysha chuckled. "Oh, what's the difference?"

Owen glanced down at her backside and laughed. "You're right: at least I still have something covering my underwear!"

Alysha felt the back of her pants and gasped. The abrupt increase of friction had ripped the seat of her jeans to shreds.

"I can't believe this. I love these jeans!" Alysha screamed. "They're my do-nothing-relaxing jeans!"

"Now they have built-in air-conditioning," Owen said with a smirk.

"That's *so* not funny," Alysha said.

Simon stopped short and put a hand to his head. The weariness was back, worse than before. He stumbled, almost falling over. Owen and Alysha both grabbed him.

"Simon!" Alysha shouted.

"Are you okay?" Owen asked.

"Yeah, I guess. I just need to get some rest."

"Controlling the laws of the universe must take a lot out of you," Owen said.

"Come on," Alysha said, "we'll walk you home. Maybe we can all meet up tomorrow and try some more formulas?" She looked from Simon to Owen hopefully.

Simon gave a tired smile, and Owen nodded. "You're on," Simon said.

THIS CHRONICLE KEEPS GETTING BETTER

This was the strangest Chronicle I'd ever narrated. I mean, Outsider children performing stunts in Dunkerhook Woods? I wasn't used to this type of work.

To be honest, my job had many drawbacks. For one thing, I had to remain cooped up in my apartment, focused on the unfolding history, for hours on end. And let's face it, observing the Order of Physics could get rather boring.

A colleague of mine assigned to the Math League told me they're an exciting lot. Granted, they all wear funny hats and thick-framed glasses and either speak in garbled English or Latin. But the League deals with theories and postulations that control the very fabric of existence. Their Keeper,

Skyrena McSteiner, guides them in controlling these at least once a month, if not more. Just imagine . . . one slip and they can unravel the entire universe!

As for Physics, Ralfagon was an affable chap to be sure, but he made everyone in his Order live close by in Lawnville, and he imposed strict regulations against them toying with reality. There were occasional field trips into space when they worked with the Order of Astronomy, but they mostly stayed in town.

To be fair, I found most Physics members colorful, likable folks, but I often longed for something new and interesting in my viewing. Distinction. Drama. Danger. Derring-do. And other things, whether they started with a *d* or not.

It looked like Simon and his friends were granting my wish.

CHAPTER 14

School's Out for Physics

It was dark inside Ralfagon Wintrofline's office at Milnes University. The only illumination came from the lamp on his desk, where he sat. He wore his overcoat indoors (he always wore it, rain or shine) and absently rubbed the metallic handle of his wooden cane. The door was again closed and sealed by powerful formulas.

I noticed that Ralfagon appeared even more distracted than he normally did. He gazed around his office and closed his eyes before speaking. "Looks good, doesn't it? Eldonna straightened up again. But a neat office doesn't change anything."

It was so dark I couldn't see who Ralfagon was speaking to, if anyone at all.

"There's no way around it now," he continued. "I have been careful, but I know something's going to happen. And soon. I can feel it."

He paused, listening. "Yes, I know," he said. "Mermon is a threat. Remember, it wasn't even my choice to let him into the Order. Just because a man gets struck by lightning twelve times and lives, those fool Board members think he might be valuable." He sighed. "But I'm not worried about Mermon; he couldn't be masterminding this. He doesn't have the intelligence."

He paused and quietly mumbled a few nonsensical words. Then he shrugged. "Who knows who's helping him? Perhaps others in the Order. That's why I can't trust anyone now. I *know* there was someone else in Dunkerhook Woods during our last meeting. I *felt* a presence. Surely, it disrupted Robertitus's formula and caused that crevice. I just don't know what or how, and without the Council's help, I can't find out."

He absently gestured with his hands and frowned. "Yes, there's that, too. An odd disturbance in the laws. Someone is using formulas in ways they shouldn't. There's a great amount of physics energy somewhere nearby that I can't explain. I know you've sensed it, too. I believe you know more about this than you're telling me . . . but it's often that way, isn't it? I understand; you have your secrets. As for me, I'm feeling old, my friend. Old and scared. My own Order may be filled with traitors, and even those who are loyal probably think I'm insane."

He listened again and then chuckled. "No, you're right; conversations like this don't help my case. Nor does my memory. That's what I get for filling my head with so many laws of physics. At least I don't dabble in theoretical physics like you! That's where the real trouble comes from." He sighed again. "But that's not important right now. What matters is *you*."

He closed his eyes and wiggled his fingers. "I want you to be ready. If something happens to me, I want you to go somewhere safe. Even if it means going far away. Or to another time. Find a place where the enemy, whoever they may be, can't get at you. Don't worry about me; this is bigger than me, old friend. This is about the universe. If something happens, don't try to be a hero. Just go. Promise me."

Ralfagon listened intently and then nodded. "Good. You'll do fine, if it comes to that." He clicked on his lamp, illuminating the whole office.

Looking around, he laughed humorlessly. "So much for a neat office, hmm? That's my worst habit of all." While he'd been talking, Ralfagon had unthinkingly mumbled a formula of motion; his casual gestures accidentally turned his clean office into an unholy mess once again.

Ralfagon stood up. "That's as good a sign as any: time to go home."

He opened his overcoat and stroked . . . the Book! There it was, dark blue cover, thick binding, the words *Teacher's Edition of Physics* printed in white.

But how? I had seen Simon using it not ten minutes earlier! Could the book be in two places at once? I wondered.

Ralfagon shuffled to his door. "Just don't forget your promise," he whispered. "Someplace safe. Or somewhen, if you must."

Ralfagon limped to the parking lot, leaning heavily on his cane. Oddly enough, he was barefoot.

"Professor Winter! Professor!" The quiet afternoon was disrupted by Eldonna's insistent shout as she waved a pair of tan construction boots: his. Ralfagon didn't even slow down. Finally, Eldonna cupped her hands around her mouth and whispered her own formula. Her voice went straight to Ralfagon's ear, boldly ignoring the fact that they were hundreds of feet apart. "Ralfagon!"

Ralfagon jerked up his head and focused on Eldonna. He whispered the same formula she had, saying, "Ah, yes. Hello, Eldonna." His reply went straight to the stout woman's ears.

She spoke back in the same fashion. "You've forgotten your shoes in your office again. I won't even mention the mess you left, too."

Ralfagon looked at his feet. "Indeed." He chuckled and started toward her.

Suddenly, he glanced around; he sensed something unusual. His eyes passed right over a pickup truck illegally parked up the sloping street; there was nobody inside. He didn't notice as the truck's stick shift started wiggling and popped into gear. The tires turned so that the truck veered into the middle of the street on a collision course with Ralfagon. The motor was off, but still the truck sped up.

"Ralfagon, look out!" Eldonna screamed, repeating her voice-throwing trick.

Ralfagon turned toward the truck and opened his mouth to say a formula; with his knowledge, he could have easily stopped the truck or turned it into a can of tomato soup. But instead, he abruptly bent over and clutched at his stomach.

"LOOK OUT!" Eldonna shouted again. This time, she didn't bother to direct her voice to him: her words split the air like a giant's roar. Every man, woman, and child on campus grabbed their ears, but that was no help to Ralfagon.

He bent over farther, grabbing at his stomach with one hand and his throat with the other. He gagged and choked, unable to move or to speak.

Eldonna sprinted across the grassy field, but she was too late. The truck smacked into Ralfagon, hurling him back several feet to slam into the pavement.

Just as the truck was about to run him over, the steering wheel turned and the truck swerved away. It bounced over the far curb and into the parking lot, smashing noisily into a parked car. Eldonna ran over to where a small crowd was gathered around Ralfagon.

As Eldonna bent over to check on her boss and Keeper, a flash of light burst out from his overcoat. The gathered people jumped back in fear, especially when they heard a bizarre ripping sound. One man sniffed and looked around. "Did someone tear open a vacuum cleaner bag?" he asked.

People shouted and a few dialed 911 on their cell phones. Eldonna knelt over Ralfagon with tears dripping from her eyes. He didn't react at all to the salty drops that splashed onto his face.

Only I noticed Mermon Veenie in the crowd around Ralfagon: he was wearing a hat, a false beard, and glasses to hide his face. He also wore a very smug smile.

WHAT CAN A NARRATOR DO?

An ambulance screeched to the scene. As paramedics rushed to aid Ralfagon, the equipment inside the open ambulance was pushed aside, as if some invisible being had climbed in. A slight suspicion crept into my head. As soon as it did, the hooded figure appeared, crouched in a corner of the ambulance. No one else seemed to notice him; Ralfagon was loaded into the vehicle, defenseless against that mysterious hooded menace.

The intruder poked delicately at Ralfagon's coat, being careful not to alert the others to his presence. That wasn't hard; they were preoccupied with keeping Ralfagon alive as they rushed to the hospital. I guessed what the hooded figure was up to: he wanted the *Teacher's Edition*. But he couldn't seem to find it! He slumped back, clearly frustrated.

Poor Simon, Alysha, and Owen had no idea what danger had befallen the Book's previous owner, and worse, they didn't know what threat might await them. I had never felt so useless, so pointless, as then. There I was, narrating with no way of aiding poor Ralfagon. Even if I broke my Society's rules forbidding interference in a Chronicle, what could I do?

I was stuck, sitting miserably in my chair, awaiting history's next chapter.

CHAPTER 15

THE DARK SIDE OF THE WOODS

That evening, Simon barely managed to stay awake through dinner. He went to sleep as soon as he was finished eating and woke up over twelve hours later. After eating a huge brunch, he waited for his two guests to arrive.

As planned, Alysha and Owen showed up at Simon's house at noon. Simon had insisted they meet there; he wasn't sure if either would be able to find the woods without him. Sure enough, Alysha and Owen remembered having gone into the woods but had no idea where it was.

"Guys, just trust me," Simon said.

Alysha and Owen exchanged a look as they followed Simon down Van Silas Way. "I think I'd remember if the forest was *here*, Simon," Alysha said. "I mean, those trees were huge! We'd be able to see them from school, wouldn't we?"

Owen nodded sadly. "I hate to say it, but she's right: there's nothing here." They reached the end of the street. "Just a dead end."

Simon smiled. "Uh-huh. Right." Then he grabbed their arms and tugged them forward. Before Alysha or Owen could protest, they'd stumbled up the curb and across the threshold.

Once again, they experienced the miraculous: the world around them was suddenly filled with towering trees, wild and vibrant foliage, and air that tasted better than ice cream sundaes.

"Ah, it's good to be back," Alysha said.

"Sure is," Owen agreed, as if they'd known the woods were there all along.

Simon stared at Alysha and Owen. "Whatever's scrambling their brains *can't* be healthy," he mumbled. Then the Breeze washed over his friends and him, and he sighed. "But that wind makes it all worthwhile."

On the way to the clearing, Simon stopped short as he spotted the bird again. There it was, on a tree branch above him. That pesky sparrow had stalked him most of the week. This time, it was with a cluster of sparrows, all chattering away in that piercing way sparrows had. Simon wondered if the spy sparrow had brought the other birds along so it could try to blend in.

Its white stripe still set it apart, though. Simon noticed it stealing glances at him from time to time. Then it froze, cocked its head to the side, and chirped loudly. It must have been some bird command because all the other birds fell silent.

Simon gaped, and Alysha and Owen took notice.

"That was weird," Alysha said. "Look at those birds flying off!"

Simon frowned. *All but one*, he thought. *All but the spy.* Just then, the sound of angry voices broke out farther down the path.

"I hear something growly, like a lion speaking English!" Owen said.

Alysha frowned. "Yeah, it sounds pretty creepy."

Simon shuddered at the mean-sounding voice. "Who talks like that?"

"Why don't we guess *after* we hide for a bit?" Owen asked. "Just to be sure."

Simon glanced at the bird, which clearly nodded, like it was agreeing with Owen. "Okay. Let's go behind those bushes, just in case."

The trio stepped out of the clearing. Owen winced at every crumpling leaf or crackling branch until they crouched down behind a row of thick bushes. They peeked through the branches and watched the clearing.

I focused my attention closer to the entrance to the woods. Mermon Veenie was walking along, neatly dressed in a tailored blue suit. The fact that he wasn't wearing a raincoat meant he must not have come through the Gateway.

Oddly, he seemed to be talking to himself. He was gesturing, too, but I could see nobody around him. Then I thought of the hooded figure, and once again, as if my thoughts had conjured him up, he appeared in that long, black hooded coat, walking alongside Veenie.

"I watched carefully at the crash site, Sir," Mermon said in his gruff, gravelly voice. "Eldonna took nothing. I don't see how she could have the Book. You searched his coat and I checked his office. Nothing. It can only be here."

The booming voice split the air in response to Veenie. **"Of course it must be here. It *was* my idea to come, wasn't it?"**

Simon, Alysha, and Owen covered their mouths to keep from crying out. To them, the hooded figure had appeared out of nowhere when his voice rang out.

"Yes, Sir," Mermon said. "Sorry, Sir. Since we're alone in Dunkerhook Woods, could you please take the hood off? It makes your voice so loud."

The hooded figure shook his head. **"No. I prefer to remain hooded for now so I can avoid that Dunkerhook Breeze."**

Mermon frowned. "But, Sir . . . wouldn't the Breeze help with your pain?"

The hooded figure snaked gloved hands under his thick coat sleeves and scratched at his arms. I caught a glimpse of them: they were slender and coated in tattoos of varying colors. **"My pain is considerable, yes. But it is a burden I have chosen: a badge of pride. And I will be able to lessen it soon enough, once I have the Book."**

They arrived at the clearing. **"I shall begin looking by Ralfagon's stump,"** the hooded figure said. **"Perhaps he had some secret storage spot there."**

"You are probably right, Sir. Funny thing, though—I am certain I heard a man near the accident site say something about a vacuum cleaner bag. Was that from something you did, Sir?"

There was a long pause as the deep, dark hood opening was fixed upon Mermon. **"Veenie, you fool!"** the echoing voice boomed. **"You just now mention this to me?"**

Mermon's harsh voice struggled to sound apologetic. "Sir, I didn't notice anything important about it!"

"The smell of a vacuum cleaner bag, where there was clearly no vacuum cleaner, could only be the stink of time and space bending! Ralfagon's last conscious act must have been to send the Book away through space and time. It could be any-where. Worse, it could be any*when*!"

Mermon hung his head, quivering with fear. Whoever this hooded figure was, his power was enough to terrify the vicious Veenie. "I am so sorry, Sir, I had no idea. My formula has nothing to do with time or space. How could I know?"

The hooded figure nodded. **"Yes, yes. Your igno-**

rance is astounding. **Ralfagon kept the greatest powers hidden from his Order, which is why you are aiding me, isn't it?"**

"Yes, Sir. I like power very much. But I also hate Ralfagon. I would gladly see that old fool dead." He coughed. "On that note, Sir, I'm puzzled. Why didn't you want Ralfagon killed yesterday?"

The hooded figure swiveled his head to stare Mermon in the face. **"Are you questioning my judgment, Veenie?"**

Mermon's tiny black dot eyes managed to widen into larger black dots. "No, no, no, Sir. I was just . . . curious."

"Curiosity is a good thing, like onion soup. But too much onion soup makes your breath smell terrible. And too much curiosity can make your whole body smell terrible, if it causes you to be dead."

Veenie nodded carefully; it was a strange threat, but a threat nonetheless. "Yes, Sir. Sorry, Sir."

The hooded figure waved a hand in dismissal. **"I'm sure you are. Don't worry about my plans for Ralfagon. I have reasons, I assure you."** The hooded figure continued to walk around Ralfagon's stump, poking at it with gloved hands.

Mermon roamed around the cluster of shorter stumps, soon passing near the kids' hiding spot. Suddenly he squinted, his eyes shrinking even smaller (impossible as that seemed) while he scratched his slicked-back hair. "Sir? I . . . ummm . . ."

The hooded figure uttered a loud, rude word. **"Veenie,"** he said, **"I told you to go before we left!"**

"No, Sir, not that. There's something you should see."

The hooded figure didn't bother to turn around. **"If it isn't the Book, I don't care."**

Mermon frowned; he scratched his head again. "Oh." He paused. "But, Sir . . ."

A loud sigh echoed out from the hood. **"What, Veenie? What is so important that you would risk my wrath again?"**

Mermon Veenie pointed in the direction of the shrubs where Simon, Owen, and Alysha were hiding. "One of those bushes is trembling."

CHAPTER 16

THE HOOD COMES OFF
(AND SPARKS FLY)

The bush Owen was hiding behind started to shake harder. Alysha and Simon grabbed him to make him stop trembling, but that only made their bushes rustle, too.

"There, do you see it, Sir? That's odd behavior for bushes, don't you think?"

"Odd behavior for bushes? You need to start using a less toxic hair gel." The hooded figure walked to Veenie and looked at the bushes. **"Stupid hood ruins my depth perception."**

With that, he pulled back the enormous hood. Shockingly, the hooded figure was really an un-hooded woman. A beautiful one with sharp green eyes and shoulder-length hair so brightly golden it almost shimmered.

"Much better," the woman said. Without the hood, her voice was sweet and melodic. She squinted at the bushes. "Now let's see . . ." She pulled up one sleeve of her black coat and glanced at a series of different-colored squiggles and shapes that were tattooed along her arm. They clearly weren't normal, though. They were so vivid and almost three-dimensional that they seemed alive instead of just ink.

"Where did I put it?" she asked. "I tell you, Veenie, these tattoos are almost more trouble than they're worth. Forget the strain of bearing them; simply finding them is a horror." She frowned as she twisted her arm to check by her elbow, then switched arms and scanned the squiggles there. "Aha, here we go."

She stared at a vibrant yellow tattoo—a set of thick, sharp-pointed lines and small circles—that virtually pulsated on her shoulder. She spoke several bizarre words, but the process was nothing like the peanut buttery sound of the Orders' formulas: it sounded more like the woman was speaking while chewing glass. The tattoo glowed brightly for an instant, and the whole field of bushes' leaves crumbled into bitter-smelling ash. The woman winced but nodded in satisfaction.

I dropped my jaw in disbelief. I mean, it was still attached to my head, but my mouth fell open. Nobody, in the many, many centuries since the Knowledge Union first formed, had ever made a formula into a tattoo. Yet she had just enacted a Chemistry command from one. She had several more on both arms, and as each tattoo's color indicated, they were from several different Orders. I saw more yellow for Chemistry, as well as blue for Physics, green for Biology, and even silver for Astronomy.

The woman leaned forward and smiled at Simon, Alysha, and Owen huddling behind the bare bushes. "And who have we here?"

Mermon sputtered. "Outsiders? How? Dunkerhook Woods has safeguards!"

The no-longer-hooded woman glanced at Mermon. "I found a way around some of the Union's rules; why couldn't others? Though I am surprised that children managed it."

She glanced at the kids and frowned. "Mermon, find out what they're doing here," she said in a bored tone.

Mermon bent forward, lowering his beady eyes toward them. "You punks!" His growling voice became a low roar, and the kids cowered. "What are you doing here? Tell me before I tear you apart!"

The woman sighed. "Veenie, behave. They're not in boot camp. Step aside." She frowned and snapped her fingers. "Hi, kids. So, explanation. Why are you here?" Her voice was gentler than Mermon's, but her tone was firm.

Alysha stood up from her crouched position and, I noticed, clenched her knees together to stop them from shaking. "Why are *we* here? Just who do you two think you are? We came in here to have some privacy, thank you very much. Why don't you and Señor Growl Face get lost before we tell the police that two strangers came after us in the woods!"

The woman chuckled. "I doubt anyone would understand what you meant if you mentioned these woods." She gestured around her. "You shouldn't even know they're here." She paused. "You are right about one thing—there's no need to be strangers. Why don't your friends join the conversation?"

Simon tugged at Owen's sleeve, and they both stood up next to Alysha; the Book was safely hidden in Simon's backpack.

"'Bout time; ever hear of chivalry?" Alysha muttered.

The woman tossed back her beautiful hair and smiled, but it was a cold smile; she looked as friendly as a crocodile before it took a nibble. "Now, as I was saying, let's be friends. My name is Sirabetta, but you can call me Sir if you want. All my friends do; I insist upon it. My associate, Mermon Veenie, and I are looking for a big blue book. It would bore you with all its dull science information, but it's very important to us. Have you seen it?"

"Look, See-ruh-whatever," Alysha said, "I don't know what you know about kids, but on weekends, we try to get away from books and school. I mean, reading on a Saturday? Please!"

Simon and Owen glanced at Alysha, impressed by her display of attitude.

Sirabetta frowned; she didn't seem as impressed. "Our Book. You. Seen it?"

Alysha rolled her eyes while Simon and Owen just shook their heads. "If you're not going to leave, we will," she said. "We have better things to do, right, boys?" Without waiting for an answer, Alysha put a hand on each boy's shoulder and turned them away.

"Good," Mermon growled, loud enough for the kids to hear. "Let's get them out of here so we can keep searching."

"Fool," Sirabetta hissed. "Did you ever think that they might be lying?"

"Sir . . . why would children want it?" Mermon asked. "It looks like a schoolbook, and they wouldn't be able to even open it."

"Why?" Sirabetta shouted. "Who knows? But *that* one has a backpack which is the *perfect* size to hold the Book. Furthermore, they weren't surprised by those leaves miraculously disappearing." She arched an eyebrow. "Either they've been around some very rare foliage, or they know something. Veenie, show them what happens if I get upset."

Mermon nodded and spoke a formula. He held his hands in front of him, and they gave off a bright blue-and-white glow. There was a loud humming like a guitar amplifier being switched on, and then a thick, blue-white bolt of lightning roared out of his fingertips.

The kids jumped as the lightning streaked past them, splitting the air with a terrible roar of thunder before shattering the trunk of a small tree.

Sirabetta smiled coldly as the kids huddled together. "That was a warning shot. Now. One more time. Are you going to tell me what you know, or does Veenie make you extra-crispy?"

CHAPTER 17

WEAPONS OF WAR

Simon, Owen, and Alysha stared at the shards of wood that had flown from the ruined, smoking tree trunk.

The silence was broken by Alysha, who cleared her throat loudly. "Okay, we're sorry, please hold on!" she said politely. She held up her hands above her head. "Simon, friction!" she hissed.

Simon faked a cough. "But we'll have to get to the trail first," he muttered, with his hands covering his mouth.

He forced himself to calm down and think. He'd read countless books about heroes facing terrible danger. They always made it seem so easy, like the answers just dropped from the sky—

His eyes widened. "I've got it; just get ready to do what I do," he whispered urgently.

Sirabetta stared at them from the edge of the clearing; her beautiful features were twisted into an angry frown. "I give you a chance to live and you use it to whisper with one another?" She shook her head. "Veenie, would you like to turn one of them into charcoal? Perhaps the smallest?"

"That's me!" Owen whimpered.

"Okay, okay," Simon shouted. "We'll come out; don't shoot. Er, whatever."

Sirabetta snapped her fingers. "Then get over here right now!"

Simon deliberately made his voice whiny. "First, keep that scary guy away!"

Sirabetta rolled her eyes so well, she made Alysha look like an amateur. "Veenie, step back from the bushes."

"You, too," Simon shouted.

Sirabetta arched an eyebrow. "Fine, but don't try anything stupid. You can't outrun a bolt of lightning."

Sirabetta and Veenie backed away across the clearing without taking their eyes off the kids. Simon, Alysha, and Owen walked through the barren shrubs.

"Now, start talking," Sirabetta said. "Tell me what you know about the *Teacher's Edition of Physics*."

Simon couldn't help but smile. That was the perfect setup for a heroic line. "Tell you? I'll show you." Then he pointed at

Veenie and Sirabetta while he spoke the gravity formula. Mermon and Sirabetta looked at each other, baffled.

Before they could react, Simon ducked down and grabbed two handfuls of rocks from the forest floor; Owen and Alysha did the same. Simon threw his rocks at Sirabetta's and Veenie's feet, and Alysha and Owen followed his lead. Sirabetta and Veenie jumped back to avoid being hit by the rocks, just as Simon hoped they would.

When they pushed off the ground, they kept floating upward. Mermon waved his arms and legs, yelping, but Sirabetta caught on instantly. "He's made us weightless—they have the Book!"

Simon then spoke a different version of the gravity formula, and the villains were hurled back at a thick tree behind them. Thanks to Simon's words, they were falling toward the tree as if it were the ground.

Mermon slammed into the trunk and was pinned several feet above the dirt floor. He didn't move; the impact had stunned him.

Sirabetta, however, quickly pulled up the other sleeve of her long black coat as she soared back. There were several more formula tattoos on that arm; she immediately found and read a blue formula on her forearm. She stopped in midair, just inches from the tree.

Simon rephrased his formula so the gravitational pull on her became ten times more than normal. Sirabetta thudded into the tree for a second but, with obvious strain, pulled slowly away from the trunk. She was able to resist Simon's formula!

Simon saw this and gulped. "We've got to go!" he yelled to Alysha and Owen. "Brace yourselves; you've got to keep your balance."

Simon spoke another formula and altered the friction of their feet, giving their toes enough resistance to let them push off and control their speed. "Remember, this is like ice-skating."

"I don't know how to ice-skate," Owen said, moaning.

Alysha grabbed his arm. "You're about to learn." The three pushed off and started sliding through the clearing and back along the path toward Van Silas Way. The Breeze blew again, this time pushing Simon and his friends along and flooding them with energy to help them escape. They needed it.

Simon risked a look backward and saw Sirabetta, still somehow fighting the pull of ten g's. She was slowly lowering herself toward the ground.

He focused on keeping his balance as he and his friends zoomed off the curb onto Van Silas Way. He heard an angry scream and several loud explosions ring out from the woods.

Simon saw Alysha start to turn her head. "Don't look back!" he shouted. "Just get to my house!"

The kids slid up Jerome Street, pausing to help Owen each time he slipped and fell. They whooshed to Simon's doorway, and Simon reversed the friction formula so they could walk normally. They rushed inside, and he double-bolted the door behind them.

It was only a temporary fix, though. If Sirabetta and Mermon Veenie figured out where they were, no doors could protect them.

CHAPTER 18

THE SPY REVEALED

Simon, Alysha, and Owen gasped for breath. "Simon, get your parents," Alysha said. "The cops'll be more likely to listen to them than to three kids."

"They're not home," Simon said. "Besides, what would we say? If I told them some evil, tattooed witch was after us, they'd probably put me on medication."

"What–do–we–do? We–have–to–call–someone–the–cops–or–the–marines–or–something," Owen whimpered.

Simon shook his head. "Nobody would believe us." He looked back at the door. "Come on, let's hide out in the basement."

He led them down the carpeted stairs, taking care to shut

the door very quietly behind them. They pushed a wooden bench to the far wall and stood on it so they could peek out through a window. The window was just above ground level and behind a row of bushes; the kids could see as far as the street, but somebody outside wouldn't be likely to notice them.

After a few minutes, Owen groaned. "My feet are starting to hurt."

"This is stupid," Alysha said. "She's probably still searching the woods."

Simon shook his head. "Sirabetta saw us running toward the street; she'll know we left. Just hope she doesn't figure out where I live."

Alysha suddenly cupped a hand over her mouth to stifle a shriek. There, a few feet away from the window, were two black boots poking out beneath a long, black coat: Sirabetta's. Fortunately, the boots were on the other side of the bushes, pointing away from the window. She was looking out onto the street.

Sirabetta made a gesture, and the kids saw Mermon Veenie coming toward her. Then the two walked back toward Van Silas Way.

Minutes later, they saw Mermon behind the wheel of a shiny red car that he must have parked on Van Silas before going to the woods earlier. He drove slowly, searching out the window. Sirabetta, sitting in the backseat, did the same, but apparently neither noticed three pairs of eyes watching from the basement window. After a moment, the car turned onto the next street.

Simon exhaled with relief. "Now what?"

"Now we get rid of the Book and give up on the woods," Owen squeaked.

"Are you nuts?" Alysha demanded. "Why?"

"Why? Why?" Owen's voice rose with every word. "Because some crazy tattooed sorceress and her growling wizard pal want to kill us." He took a breath, his voice hoarse. "Kill as in dead as in corpse as in NO WAY!"

"Stop shouting at me!" Alysha shouted back.

"Easy, guys. Relax," Simon said.

"Yeah, listen to Simon," Alysha said. "We're fine. We got away; they don't know who we are or where we live. Plus, we beat them once. We can do it again."

"*We* didn't do anything!" Owen sputtered. "Simon did it and just barely! I'm sorry, Simon, but this isn't like the books you love or the alien wizard stuff you were joking about in the woods! This is real and it's awful and it's not a game." He took a deep breath. "One of them threw lightning. Real lightning. I'm scared of thunder, and that's just sound; I mean, how are you supposed to fight lightning? If we get rid of the Book, they won't have any reason to want us."

Alysha shook her head. "We can't get rid of the Book. What if we give it to them and they come after us for revenge? Or because they don't want to leave any witnesses?

Or just because they're bad people? That Book gives us a chance. Without it, we're toast. Burnt toast."

Owen hopped off the bench and walked to the middle of the basement. "What do you even care? It's not like you're our friend; why are you even here?"

"I could be your friend," she said. "What's wrong with that?"

"People like you aren't friends with kids like us," Owen said. "You're popular and cool." He tugged at his plain T-shirt. "This is me; nothing special. Why would you want to be my friend? And you've had the locker next to Simon for how long? Why are you suddenly his friend now? You followed us because he pulled some trick in the hall and you wanted to know how. Now you know. What's keeping you here?"

Simon raised his eyebrows; he wondered that, too.

Alysha looked away and then turned back angrily. "Fine, I'll tell you. Because you're not like Marcus and Rachelle and all those others. I like that I have a lot of friends and yeah, they can be fun, but sometimes I don't think I belong with them. Owen, I didn't know you before yesterday, and you can be . . . different sometimes. But you're nice and funny. And Simon . . . well, we used to have fun, didn't we? You were always more interesting than Marcus and those guys."

She frowned and went on. "And yeah, seeing Simon using his gravity formula in the hall made me want to follow

him. But it's more. You both have a whole thing about you."
She waved her hands in the air. "Maybe it's the woods.
Maybe it changes you. Like the Book—it's magic. Real magic.
Something unique, something more special than anything
I've ever seen or heard of in real life."

Before Simon or Owen could respond, a sharp tapping
on the window made all three of them jump. It was the small
brown bird with a horizontal stripe across its belly.

Simon pointed. "It's the spy!" he gasped. "He's been following me practically all week!"

"A bird spy?" Owen looked shocked.

"Let him in and see what he wants," Alysha said. She
stretched up on the bench to unlatch the window.

Owen grabbed her arm. "Let him in? Are you nuts?" At
her warning look, he quickly let go but said, "What–if–he–is–
a–spy–or–some–kind–of–killer–bird!" He took a breath.
"Haven't you seen that Alfred Hitchcock movie *The Birds*?"

The bird looked skyward, shaking its head as if in exasperation.

Before Simon or Owen could say anything, Alysha
opened the window. The bird hopped onto the windowsill
and, with a quick flurry of its wings, landed on the basement
floor.

It chirped loudly at Owen, who ran to the other side of
the basement and hid behind one of the many file cabinets
that lined the wall. Simon reached over and flicked on a light
switch, giving them a good look at the tiny creature.

The bird flapped its wings once, twice. Then its whole body shimmered, shook, and blurred. Simon, Alysha, and Owen (watching with his fingers spread over his eyes) gawked as the tiny bird transformed into a tall, skinny man with short brown hair. He appeared to be in his midtwenties and was dressed in brown pants and a long-sleeved brown-and-gray shirt with a horizontal white stripe in the middle.

The man nodded politely at Simon and Alysha, then turned to Owen and shook his head. "*The Birds?* Stick to watching cartoons, Courageous Cat."

His voice was smooth and fast, like he was on the verge of breaking into song.

Simon and Alysha stepped down from the bench. "Who are you?" Simon asked, his voice tinged with awe. "And how did you do that?"

"You can call me Flangelo Squicconi, little Newton," the bird man said. "I've come from the Order of Biology, and you've got some explaining to do."

CHAPTER 19

FROM THE MOUTHS OF BIRDS

Simon blinked. "Wait . . . the Order of what? Flannel who?"

"Oh, you're a special boy, aren't you?" Flangelo said. "Listen carefully." He pointed at himself. "My name is Flan–jell–oh Skwi–cho–knee. I can write it for you if it'll help. And I'm here from the Order of Bye–ahl–oh–jee." He paused. "It's a science." He paused again while the trio just stared at him. "Study of living things." He sighed. "This is going to be one of those days, isn't it?"

Alysha put her hands on her hips. "Yeah, we know what biology is, and we understand what you want, but we have our own questions. Like what is the Order of Biology and how did you turn from Tweety Bird into a real live boy?"

"Ooooh, sassy." Flangelo clapped. "The Order of Biology is just like your Order of Physics, only we practice biology, not physics, get it? I saw what just happened in your Dunkerhook Woods, and I want to know just what you junior scientists are up to, pronto." He snapped his fingers several times.

Alysha stomped her foot. "Are you threatening us? You saw how we handled those two back in the woods."

Flangelo sneered. "Yes, that was very energetic running you did. Bravo."

"That's it," Alysha said. "Simon, use the fireball and flame-broil him."

Flangelo's face went pale. "Okay, okay, no need to get pushy. I'm not here for trouble, just information."

"You *are* a spy!" Owen gasped.

Flangelo waved him away. "Hush, field mouse. I'm no spy, just an emissary."

"Emi-what?" Alysha asked.

Flangelo looked up at the sky in exasperation. "I'll bet you all rule at Scrabble. *Emissary*. It means 'messenger.'"

Alysha gestured for him to continue.

Flangelo cleared his throat. "I'm a *messenger* for Gilio Skidowsa, Keeper of the Biology's *Teacher's Edition* and head of the Order of Biology."

"Who?" all three kids asked at the same time.

Flangelo dramatically dropped his head into his hands and then looked up with a frown. "My boss. Leader of Biology. He has a Book just like Ralfagon Wintrofline's, only it says *Biology* on the cover."

Simon pulled the Book out of his backpack. "You mean like this?"

Owen gasped. "Simon–don't–let–him–see–it–he'll–attack–us–too!"

"Who, Robin the Bird Wonder?" Alysha laughed. "What's he going to do, chirp us to death?"

Flangelo folded his arms. "Well, there's no need to be so rude about it. I mean, Robin? Green shorts? Tights? Please. Besides, I've already seen you with the Book. My question is, why do you have it? Where's Ralfagon?"

"That was the name in the Book!" Simon said. "Who is he?"

Flangelo made a trilling noise. "Who is–? Are you sure that lightning missed you?" Under his breath, he muttered, "That would explain a lot, actually."

"Watch it, feathers," Alysha said.

"Let's start simply," Flangelo said. "What are your names?"

"I'm Simon; this is Alysha and Owen."

Flangelo trilled again. "Those are completely normal names! You–" He gasped. "You're not in the Order, are you?"

Simon shrugged. "Which Order, exactly?"

"Oh no," Flangelo warbled. "I've been afraid of this since I started watching you. You're not even in the Knowledge Union. You're Outsiders!"

"Please, just tell us what's going on," Simon said.

Flangelo sighed. "I'll bet you can't throw fireballs, can you?" When Simon shook his head, Flangelo glared at Alysha. "Flame-broiled, huh? Big faker."

"I don't know why the Book came to me, but it calls me Keeper," Simon said.

"This makes no sense," Flangelo said. "You see, Gilio sent me to check on Ralfagon and his Order."

"How is that not spying?" Alysha demanded.

"Gilio and Ralfagon are friends," Flangelo said. "It's different when you watch over friends. Gilio wanted me to find out what the Order of Physics did after the Council was forced to disband." He raised a finger to stop Alysha from asking. "The Council of Sciences is all the Keepers—the leaders—of the Science Orders. Which are the folks with science-related Books. Like yours."

"So what did you find out?" Simon asked.

"I've been flying around the town and the woods all week. I saw you and Squeaky Boy coming out of the woods with the *Teacher's Edition* on Tuesday, which made no sense. I checked on Ralfagon that same night, and he was perfectly healthy, so I started following you." He chirped nervously. "But now that crazy duo says they put Ralfagon in the hospital. They're blowing things up and are oh, so very unhappy with you three. I just don't know what to do."

"Can I ask you some questions?" Alysha asked.

Flangelo sighed. "Like saying no would work?"

Alysha scrunched her brow in concentration. "So there's

a big group of people—the Knowledge Union—and some of them have Books, like Simon's *Teacher's Edition*. And they can all control different sciences?"

Flangelo nodded. "There are all sorts of groups, actually. The Orders deal with Sciences, the Guilds make things, and so on. Everything that makes the universe tick has a group, and it's all watched over by the Board of Administration. They're the ultimate bureaucracy." He saw their confused expressions. "Think about all the headaches your parents have with waiting in line at the Department of Motor Vehicles or filing taxes. Picture that, only the BOA is in charge of people who can control existence. They're experts at putting the squeeze on, I tell you." He chuckled, and then noticed the kids' blank faces. "Never mind."

"You mean there's all this stuff going on right around us? All the time?" Simon asked.

"Since the dawn of humanity, there's been a Knowledge Union," Flangelo explained. "Maybe even before, with the dolphins or something." He stood proudly. "Biology deals with evolution, you know." Seeing the kids' blank looks again, he sighed. "Can you even walk and chew gum at the same time?"

"You know," Simon replied, "this *is* a lot to absorb. You could be nicer."

"Yeah," Alysha said, "if someone's going to insult these guys, I'd prefer it was me." She saw Simon's look and smiled. "Kidding."

"Listen, I'm sorry, kids. Really," Flangelo said in a kinder tone. "But I'm pretty confused myself. I'm somewhat new to the Order of Biology, so I don't understand how everything works. I don't even know what to do about reporting this whole mess with Ralfagon and the Book."

"Why not call Gilio on the phone and ask for advice?" Simon asked.

"Oh, if only it was that easy," Flangelo trilled. "Gilio hates technology; he doesn't trust it. Thinks it's too easy to fake or trace phone calls, faxes, e-mails, and so on. You should hear his conspiracy theories. He's more cuckoo than I am." He whistle-laughed. "Anyhoo, that's part of why he wanted me here: he was afraid some Order members were working together to bring down the whole system."

Flangelo paused to chew on his lower lip. "Okay, maybe he wasn't so cuckoo on that one. Which is particularly bad news for you three."

Owen dragged himself out from behind the file cabinet, where he'd been hiding all along. "Bad-news-why-bad-news-for-us?"

"Look who's come to join us; welcome back," Flangelo said. "It's bad news because that tacky tattooed bleached blonde and the beady-eyed Zeus wannabe are going to do everything in their power to get that Book. Them and any-one else who's in on their conspiracy. They'll stop at nothing, and even if you give up the Book, they'll probably still elim-inate you."

Simon, Alysha, and Owen all stared in horror while Flangelo awkwardly looked away. Then he brightened. "Hey, I love this basement. Very minimalist, really. Who's your decorator?"

Owen moaned and crawled back behind the file cabinet.

Flangelo frowned. "We'll just talk when you're done hiding."

CHAPTER 20

BETTER LIVING THROUGH IMPRINTING

"So we're dead no matter what." Simon gulped. "Flangelo, will you help us?"

Flangelo sadly shook his head. "Sorry, Keeper Junior. I'm no fighter. I was just a graduate student before I joined the Order, and now, I turn into a sparrow. I chirp, I fly, I chat with birds. Ooooh, scary me."

Owen groaned loudly. "We're–dead–we're–so–dead–it's–all–over."

"This Sirabetta woman is something else," Flangelo said. "Nobody's ever done what she did."

"What, turn invisible?" Alysha asked.

Flangelo let out a whistling laugh. "Invisible? Any

Physics member with a good light formula can do that. The Bio folks have their own versions of camouflage, too. No, I meant the tattoos. As you surely know, formulas are imprinted into your brain so they can be triggered when needed. It's more instant than memory, even. Nobody but a Keeper should be able to write one down, much less tattoo it onto someone's skin. Plus, Sirabetta obviously has access to formulas from different Orders. She used Physics and Chemistry, and I'm pretty sure I saw some from Biology. That's not just dangerous; it should be impossible."

Noticing the scared looks on the kids' faces, he cleared his throat. "Look, I'm sure you'll be fine. You have the Book, you have the power; just prepare yourselves to fight the bad guys." He pointed at Simon. "Next time, have your friends chip in with their formulas, too."

"How?" Simon asked. "The Book's commands look like squiggles to them."

"Of course." Flangelo whistle-laughed. "The Book belongs to the Keeper; it's up to you to share the formulas." He saw their expressions. "What, you thought I could just naturally turn into a bird? Bitten by a sparrow on the full moon and now I'm cursed to poop on the heads of those I love the most? Oh, children, stay away from the cartoons and *use* those noggins!"

Alysha raised an eyebrow. "Wait, what formula in biology deals with becoming a bird?"

"Biology isn't as clear-cut as Physics, so it's hard to

explain," Flangelo said. Seeing the kids staring at him expectantly, he coughed nervously. "It's basically evolution. In reverse. With a twist." He paused. "It's technical. I don't want to have to explain all the mysteries of nature."

Alysha turned to Simon. "He has no idea and doesn't want to look stupid." She smirked. "Too late."

Flangelo huffed. "Big deal—so I only know the basics of imprinting."

Simon could barely contain his excitement. "So it's called imprinting?"

"You've got to show us how it works!" Alysha said.

Flangelo examined his fingernails. "And why should I? You've been anything but nice, and frankly, I *know* there'll be no fireball from Simple Simon over here."

Alysha crossed her arms, her voice growing angry. "What do you want for it?"

Flangelo twittered. "Oh, wildcat, you'll never make a negotiator. You should be buttering me up, not going into diva mode." He cleared his throat. "But it just so happens that I *do* need something. A place to roost."

The kids looked at him blankly. "Oh, New Jersey, wherefore art thy dictionaries? Roost. Perch. Sleep."

"Why do you need to roost here?" Simon asked.

"Because I'm not flying all the way back to Biology headquarters until I'm done with my investigation, and it's hard to hold on to a wallet when you turn into a bird. No dough, no hotel. Get it? I need a place to stay. I could sleep in a tree, but I'd prefer something four or five star. Preferably with room service and a view."

"Flangelo, sixth graders don't bring home strangers to sleep on the couch," Simon said. "Even *my* parents would notice that."

"Hey, I didn't say it would be easy," Flangelo chirped, "but that's my price."

Simon paused to think. "Okay, I've got someplace you can stay. Now, tell us about imprinting."

"It's simple, really. Gilio wrote out my formula with his Book's special pen on a normal piece of paper. He put my name on the page so I could read it, too; anybody else would just see squiggles. Once I read the formula over enough, it seeped into my mind. Now I can use it whenever I want. That's it."

"Thank you," Simon said. "Let me show you your roost." He led Flangelo and his friends across the basement.

Most of the file cabinets lining the walls had labels with names like Clients, Personal Records, Delivery Menus, or Label-Making Companies. But one thick and sturdy cabinet had no labels, just padlocks on each drawer.

Flangelo pointed to it. "What's in there, the Nixon tapes?" he asked.

"Who's Nixon?" Owen asked.

Flangelo shook his head. "I wouldn't want to overload your precious mental capacity, Toto." He clapped twice. "*Garçon*, my room!"

"Who's *Garçon?*" Owen whispered to Alysha as Simon led them up the stairs. Alysha just shrugged.

On the ground floor, Simon brought them to the recreation room.

Flangelo smiled as he looked around at the overstuffed armchairs, the amply padded sofa, and the wide-screen television set. "My, what a comfy room. Splendid! I trust you have cable?"

"Yeah," Simon said, "but it's not for you." He pulled aside a heavy curtain and slid open the glass door behind it. He led Flangelo and his friends into the backyard.

"We had a deal!" Flangelo squawked.

"Yup." Simon nodded. "And here you are, your own house."

"A birdhouse?" Flangelo warbled.

Alysha and Owen burst out laughing. "Hey," Simon said, "it's got a roof, plenty of space, and a great view of the garden. Roost away!"

Flangelo sighed. "Can I at least have a bite to eat?"

"I'm sure I can dig up something." Simon dashed into the house and came back with a box of bread crumbs. He looked at the ingredients. "Good news: these are rosemary flavored!"

Flangelo turned into a bird and fluttered into the small, wooden house. His chirps sounded very angry.

Simon led Alysha and Owen into the house and closed the glass door. "That's done. So." He looked at Owen. "I think we can agree there's no point in getting rid of the Book."

Owen shook his head. "If they want us dead with or without it, then let's learn formulas and figure out how to protect ourselves." He turned to Alysha. "Maybe if we all stick together, we can do it."

Alysha smiled at him. It was probably the closest Owen would come to welcoming her aboard.

Simon held up the Book. "You know, choosing good formulas could take a while. This stuff is pretty complicated."

"My sister Mona's in high school," Alysha said. "She's taking physics now, and I'll bet she has one of those books of science for dummies."

"You think?" Simon asked.

"Mona?" Alysha rolled her eyes. "Trust me, she needs it."

"I don't even know if we should be going outside," Simon said. "What if we run into Sirabetta and Mermon?"

"As long as we're careful, we'll be fine; they can't be everywhere," Owen said.

"Whoa . . . listen to you!" Alysha said. "When did you get so brave?"

Owen laughed. "Are you kidding? I'm still scared of that bird guy! But if we get our own formulas, we can kick butt!"

They hurried through town, staying alert as they went. They cut through Town Plaza, the perfect place to avoid getting noticed by bad guys. It was the busiest part of Lawnville, especially on weekends; the kids would be hard to spot in the crowd.

"Hey, want to stop for a slice first?" Simon asked as they approached Nezzo's. "A snack to keep us fueled?"

Owen looked in through the big glass storefront and gasped. "No! Let's get out of here!" He leapt away from the window. Simon and Alysha ducked down.

"Is it them?" Simon hissed. "Mermon and Sirabetta?"

Owen shook his head. "Worse! Marcus, Barry, Rachelle—all of 'em!"

Alysha rolled her eyes. "Big deal." She started to stand up. "You know, you really scared me."

As she stood, Simon and Owen both said, "Stay down!"

"Alysha, trust me, Owen does not have an easy time with those guys," Simon said in a quiet voice. "Please, just stay low."

Alysha nodded, and Simon grabbed her arm to pull her past the window.

As they snuck by, none of them realized that Marcus had spotted them and was glaring.

Alysha led Owen and Simon out of Town Plaza and into her neighborhood. Soon she pointed to a big white house. "Here it is. Home sweet home."

They followed Alysha in, down a hallway to a spacious TV room. Alysha's father was sitting there on a sofa. He looked up and smiled.

"Hi, honey. Good day?"

Alysha shrugged. "Same old, really. You remember

Simon? And this is Owen. We're going to work on a project for science in the basement."

Max Davis whistled. "On a Saturday, no less. I'm impressed."

Alysha took them through the kitchen, where they grabbed snacks and drinks, and then brought them down-stairs. Alysha ran back up while Owen and Simon oohed and aahed over the dartboard, billiards, and air hockey tables.

"Can we make this place our secret headquarters?" Owen asked when Alysha returned.

Alysha rolled her eyes. "Playtime's later, boys; I want to get cracking on this formula business. We're just lucky Mona isn't home." She held up her sister's *Physics for the Doofus* book.

Simon pulled the Book out of his backpack and placed it on the wet bar. The Book, responding to his touch, opened its clasp with a click. Simon cleared his throat. "Hello, Book. I'd like to share some formulas with Alysha and Owen if that's okay with you."

Alysha snickered. "Is that how you talk to it?"

Then Owen and Alysha gasped as the Book's cover flipped open by itself. Words, written in neat blue handwrit-ing, appeared before their eyes.

Welcome, Keeper. Do you have paper?

Simon smiled proudly while Owen took a small step back. Alysha pulled a stack of paper out of a nearby drawer.

The Book apparently sensed this because another message appeared. *Unlike the Keeper, Alysha and Owen may only have one formula each for now. Choose carefully. Also remember, Outsider science books are not completely accurate about the true laws.*

The pen rose up from the cover, making Alysha's and Owen's jaws drop.

"Thanks, Book," Simon said, giving its spine a gentle stroke. It wiggled contentedly. He took the pen and turned to Alysha and Owen. "So, what part of the universe do you guys want to control?"

They took their time, paging through the various chapters in *Physics for the Doofus* and checking them against the chapters in the *Teacher's Edition*. The Book had commands for everything in *Physics for the Doofus* and much more. There were even entire sections that *Physics for the Doofus* was missing.

Plus, the *Teacher's Edition* had different, deeper information about various laws and formulas. Alysha and Owen had a hard time understanding some of the material, much less deciding what they wanted to use.

"I think we can skip the really confusing chapters like 'Quantum Physics' and `Theoretical Physics,'" Simon said. "Why not look for something that can be used as both an offense and a defense?"

"I've got it!" Alysha said. "The perfect thing, especially for what's his name . . . Mermon Veenie." She pointed to a paragraph. "Capacitance. It's all about how much electricity an object can store up. I think I'll be like a superbattery. I should be able to absorb Veenie's lightning so he can't blow us up."

Simon pointed to some squiggles in the Book. "It says here that electrical power can be found in almost everything; something about moving electrons around. It goes on and on about atoms, too. But according to this, you can also control current. When you learn these symbols, you won't just be a battery, you'll be able to release the energy! You'll be like an electric eel. Except not in the water."

"And with arms and legs," Owen added with a smile. Alysha rolled her eyes.

Using the Book's pen, Simon copied the proper command words onto a sheet of paper. Alysha stared at it blankly.

"Oops, forgot," Simon said. He wrote Alysha's full name on the top of the page, and it glowed bright blue for a second before becoming normal ink.

Owen frowned. "Still looks like squiggles to me."

"Not to me," Alysha said. She took the page and went off to memorize it.

Simon turned to Owen. "Any ideas?"

"I dunno. I just don't want to be scared anymore."

"I don't think there's anything you can do about that," Simon said. "I mean, I have gravity and friction and I was still scared with Mermon and Sirabetta. But Alysha stood up to Sirabetta without a single formula to help her."

"Yeah, that was amazing."

"The only difference between you and me," Simon explained, "is that I told myself I wouldn't let my fear paralyze me. I kept my head working."

Owen nodded. "It does feel like paralysis. I freeze up and can't move."

Alysha called over from her corner, "It's pretty ironic, really. Normally you're a regular velocity boy."

"Ferocity boy?" Owen asked. "Huh?"

Alysha shook her head. "Velocity; you know, fast."

"Wait," Owen said. He started flipping through *Physics for the Doofus*. "Here it is: velocity, the speed and direction of an object. Alysha, you're a genius!"

"Duh!"

Owen turned to Simon. "I could move things around and control how fast they go! Even if I freeze up, I can make sure I can still move, and if someone tries to come after me, I can make sure that he can't."

Simon looked in the Book and found the special words for velocity control. "There's a lot more that you can do with it, Owen. You'll see when you memorize it." Simon wrote the symbols out for Owen, remembering to put his name on the top of the page. Then Owen went off to learn it.

Simon looked at his two new friends hunched over their sheets of paper as they absorbed the formulas. They should be ready for anything.

But in the back of his mind, he had to wonder . . . would that be enough?

CHAPTER 21

OUT OF THE FIRE

AND INTO THE FIGHT

"I've got it," Alysha called out. "I read it a few times, and get this . . . it disappeared from the paper!" Indeed, the page was now blank. "I can feel it in my head. It's amazing. And you're right, Simon: there's electrical energy everywhere. I can sense it!"

Simon felt a buzzing in his head; he looked over to the Book and got the feeling it was calling to him. When he approached, it flipped itself to the inside cover, where another glowing blue message waited for him.

Be sure to warn your friends of the weariness they will face from formula use. They will need plenty of rest and food, too.

Simon passed on the warning to Alysha and Owen

and then turned back to the Book. "Hey, did you call me over here?"

The old message had already disappeared, and a new one formed. *As our bond deepens, so will our ability to communicate. Soon, you won't have to rely on reading my messages. You will hear them in your mind.*

"Cool. Just don't go poking around in there too much, okay?"

As you wish, Keeper.

"I think I've got mine imprinted," Owen said. He looked at the page, and as with Alysha's, the formula and his name faded. "She's right! It's inside me now. I can close my eyes and feel where everything is and how it's moving—a fly in the corner over there, even my hand." He waved his hand around in front of his face, staring at it with fascination.

"I'm ready to give you guys a demonstration of my formula," Alysha said.

"Yeah, but be careful," Simon warned. "You don't want to overdo it."

"We've got to practice, right?" Alysha said. She spoke her formula. "Check this out: I can just set the formula going and start storing up electrical energy." She kicked off her shoes and walked around in socks, dragging her feet along the carpet to build up static electricity.

"So you touch metal and get a spark?" Owen asked. "Big deal; I can do that."

Alysha shook her head. "Slow down there, Speedy. Can

you do this?" She unplugged the air hockey table from the wall outlet and spoke her formula in a different way. Electricity flowed out of her hand and into the plug. The table's air jets turned on, making the plastic puck float above the table's surface. "I can feel the electricity flowing through me." She giggled. "It tickles, like really bubbly soda."

Owen walked over to the table. "Wow!"

"Let's see yours, Velocity Boy," Alysha said. "Make the puck move."

Owen closed his eyes and spoke the words. "Let's stop it first." Just like that, the puck stopped moving. The air jets were still humming, but they were no longer making the puck drift.

"Not bad, I guess," Alysha said.

Owen frowned. "Not bad? Try this." He spoke a variation on the formula, and the puck zoomed along the table, streaking into the goal near Alysha with a loud clank. He raised his arms. "Goooooooal!" he shouted.

The air jets sputtered out and Alysha frowned. "I didn't have much electricity stored up." She looked over to the outlet. "But I know where to get more!"

"NO!" Simon and Owen both shouted.

Alysha held up her hands. "I'll be fine. I can actually sense the electricity in there; I can control how much I take." She stood several feet away from the outlet and held her fingers out toward it. "I think I can just pull it out." She frowned. "Better stand back, though, just to be safe."

Simon and Owen ran over to the billiards table and crouched behind it, barely keeping their eyes above the top so they could watch.

Alysha concentrated and smiled as an arc of bluish electricity leapt from the outlet to her fingers. Holding the plug in her other hand, she focused, and the air hockey table turned back on with a whooshing noise.

Alysha smiled proudly. "See? I'm like a human power plant!"

Simon nodded as Owen and he returned to her side. "Cool."

"No, *this* is cool," Owen said as he took the puck out of the goal and put it back onto the table. Using his velocity control, he made it zigzag around the table.

"Oh yeah?" Simon said, and spoke his gravity formula. The puck suddenly became too heavy for the air jets to hold it up, and with a click, it hit the table.

Owen made a big show of cracking his knuckles. "No problem." He sent the puck sliding, only this time it made a light scraping noise.

"Hey, don't ruin the table!" Alysha said.

"Hmm." Simon spoke his friction formula, making the puck stick down. "Try and move it now!"

Owen concentrated, and the puck moved a tiny bit but then stopped again. As Simon and Owen used both their formulas on it, it moved and stopped a few more times, started to vibrate, and finally popped up into the air. When it landed, it was a mangled ball of plastic—barely recognizable as a puck.

"Guys, how am I going to explain that to my parents?" Alysha groaned.

The lights flickered, making the kids look up in alarm.

Simon frowned. "Sorry, Alysha—I guess we overdid it."

Alysha frowned. "No . . . the lights were my fault, I think."

Owen wrinkled his nose. "Anybody else smell that?"

Alysha looked down and let out a small scream. "No!" There was smoke coming from her hand and along the plastic-coated wire of the plug. "I forgot I was still giving it juice. I gave it too much!"

They all stomped on the smoldering cable, but the damage was done. The air was filled with the smell of burned plastic.

There was a knock on the basement door. "'Lysh? You okay down there?"

Alysha's father came into the basement and waved at the smoke in the air. "Are you kids okay? What happened?"

"I don't know, Dad," Alysha said. "We were just playing air hockey and the lights flickered. Next thing we knew . . ."

Max kept waving at the air. "Maybe an electrical short? You're lucky there wasn't a real fire." He stopped waving as the smoke dissipated. "Wasn't too bad; didn't even set off the smoke detector. But no more playing down here. I'm going to pull the fuses until we can get an electrician to look at the wiring."

Alysha flashed a guilty look at Simon and Owen. Simon grabbed the Book and tucked it into his backpack before Alysha's dad noticed it.

Simon and Owen followed Alysha up the stairs while Max went to the fuse box.

"Are you going to be in trouble?" Simon whispered.

Alysha shook her head. "I doubt it; it was an accident. Sort of."

Owen shrugged. "Maybe we should go."

"Guess so," Alysha said. "Let's talk later. Maybe we can meet tomorrow?"

"I think we should," Simon said.

As Simon and Owen walked down Alysha's walkway, Owen was practically exploding with excitement. "I can't believe how great this is! I have my own formula, and it is wild!"

Simon chuckled at his enthusiasm. "Yeah, but remember what the Book said. Don't go overboard with it. You don't want to get worn out, right?"

They rounded the corner and headed toward Town Plaza.

"It'll take some practicing, but we'll be ready for any-thing," Owen said.

Simon nodded. The boys walked silently for a few blocks, both lost in thought about their formulas. They were jarred by nearby chirping. It was loud and forceful, like a bird shouting.

"You think it's Flangelo?" Owen asked.

"Yup, but why is he just chattering at us?"

They squinted in the dim dusk light as they tried to find Flangelo. They finally saw him up in a small tree, waving his wings from his perch.

Simon laughed. "What's the big deal, birdie? Don't you wanna come down and talk like a person?"

Owen snickered. "What a birdbrain."

The boys laughed while Flangelo the bird glanced skyward and shook his head before resuming his frantic chirping. As Simon and Owen got closer to the tree, they heard the screech of a car's tires. They looked up and saw a shiny red car jerk to a halt a half block ahead of them.

Before the boys could react to the sight of the car, the driver-side door opened and a familiar woman dressed in a black overcoat with the hood down stepped out.

"Oh no!" Simon gasped.

"You!" Sirabetta shouted as she stormed over to them.

CHAPTER 22

THE TATTOOED LADY

Simon looked around for help, but there was nobody on the street, nobody looking through their windows, and the light was quickly fading. The boys were on their own.

Simon spoke his gravity formula, increasing Sirabetta's weight to many times normal and pinning her to the street.

"Owen, let's skate!" Simon spoke his friction formula on Owen's and his feet. "We'll go to Town Plaza—she might not attack around all those people!"

Owen recovered from his shock enough to follow Simon; they spun around and zipped down the street away from Sirabetta. They pumped their legs hard, gliding over the road and leaning carefully so as not to tip over when they streaked around a corner.

"I think we'll be okay," Simon panted. "She should be stuck for a little while."

"Wrong!" a voice shouted from above them.

They both slid to a stop and gaped. Sirabetta was soaring through the air toward them. She was free of the increased gravity, and she could fly!

Simon pointed back the way they'd come, and Owen nodded. The two started skating again, sprinting with all their might as they headed back toward Sirabetta's car.

Once again, running away didn't help—Sirabetta flew quickly and landed on the street ahead of them. They tried to reverse directions, but this time, Owen toppled over, tangling in Simon's legs and making him fall, too.

Sirabetta read a blue tattoo from one arm. It glowed brightly, and in response, a big metal mailbox on the corner blew up. Pieces of twisted metal and charred letters flew in all directions.

Simon and Owen looked up from the street, gaping in horror.

Sirabetta walked toward them. "Like that? It's one of my physics formulas; air pressure can make wonderful explosions. Now, give me the *Teacher's Edition!*"

Owen ground his teeth together. "No. Just leave us alone," he said in a trembling voice.

Simon locked eyes with Owen. "Velocity time," he mouthed.

Owen nodded and Simon whispered his formula, making Sirabetta weightless. Owen concentrated and spoke his own formula, launching Sirabetta into the sky as he increased her velocity many times. She spun end over end as she hurtled up through the air.

Simon and Owen had barely gotten to their feet when they saw the airborne Sirabetta pull up the other sleeve of her coat. A blue tattoo glowed brightly as she read it, and she halted in midair; she'd overcome Owen's formula. She swooped down to the street in front of the boys, defying Simon's formula, too.

"H-how?" Simon stammered.

"Neat trick, isn't it?" Sirabetta pointed to the glowing tattoo on her forearm. "It's a Physics formula that deals with the balance between kinetic and potential energy—energies of movement. With it, I can control my body's motion: I can fly and resist other forces, so your gravity and velocity control can't stop me."

She pulled up the bottom of her coat; her legs were covered with many more tattoos of varying colors. "On the other hand, I can do plenty to you," she said, pointing to a blue tattoo.

She read the formula, and the asphalt street melted, turning to molten tar in a wide circle around Owen and

Simon. Sirabetta smiled. "Heat. Simple but effective, no? Try sliding through that. Now . . . the *Teacher's Edition!*"

Fumes rose from the bubbling blacktop; Simon and Owen shrank away from the heat and the nostril-stinging stench coming off the road.

"But-the-Book's-Simon's-now! It-came-to-*him*-and-calls-him *Keeper!*" Owen pleaded.

Sirabetta stared for a moment, looking shocked. "What? This boy . . . is the new Keeper? He's bonded with the Book?" She snarled at Simon, "It's meant for me, not you! But while you're Keeper, I can't risk killing you. I can make your life miserable, though. Or I can take care of you like I did Ralfagon."

Then she took a deep breath, as if fighting to control her anger. When she spoke again, she sounded almost calm. "Boys, this doesn't have to be violent. If you give me the Book, I'll leave you alone. Just let me have it!"

Simon considered this for a moment, but what if she was lying? Like Alysha said, without the Book, they'd be toast. He tried stalling. "Why do you want it?"

"That's not your business. I have my needs." Sirabetta winced and scratched at the glowing blue formula.

"Do those tattoos hurt you?" Owen asked.

"Yes, they hurt, you little brat," Sirabetta snapped at him. She breathed deeply again. "These formulas aren't imprinted. I stole them, and so they rebel against me." She rubbed at the formula on her leg and groaned quietly. Her voice became almost pleading. "That's why I *need* that Book! I'll be able to imprint these Physics formulas and take some wretched tattoos off. Then I'll get Biology, Chemistry, and all the others I'll need. Then I can get what I deserve and make those fools in the Union pay for what they did!"

"What'd they do?" Simon asked.

Sirabetta shook her head. "This is not question-and-answer time. I don't want to hurt you, but I will do what is necessary; I've come too far not to." She gestured, and the intense heat from her tattoo formula spread. An even larger area of the street bubbled and burned. "I *will* get what I want."

Simon and Owen shuddered at the sight of the ruined street but didn't move.

They all turned at a honking sound. A car was driving up to them. Simon and Owen felt a quick burst of hope. Were they saved? Had help arrived?

The driver stopped and honked his horn several times. It became clear to Simon and Owen—this was just an average Outsider. He wouldn't be any help.

The man rolled down his window and stuck out his head. "Get off the road!" he yelled. He sniffed and grimaced. "Ugh, what's that smell?" He noticed the burning street and yelped. "Hey, there's a fire! Lady, get your kids off the road and get away from there!"

Sirabetta shook her head. She pulled up a sleeve and muttered, "Stupid Outsiders." She read off a formula and the pavement bucked wildly. All the garbage pails in the area toppled; several manhole covers exploded into the air and clattered loudly to the street.

The man gaped and threw his car into reverse, speeding back the way he had come.

"Simon, did–you–see, did–you–see, did–you–see?" Owen whispered.

"Yeah, I think that was the air pressure formula. We're dead meat."

"No, her formulas. Her tattoos. Look!" Owen pointed at Sirabetta's leg: the heat tattoo had stopped glowing when she used the air pressure one. "And the heat—it's gone!" He gestured to the melted street around them. The bubbling had stopped. Steam rose as the street cooled.

Simon scratched his head. "Why'd she do that?"

"She can't use two at once!" Owen whispered.

"Hey, I think you're right!"

"Enough chatting, boys," Sirabetta shouted. "Let me make this easier for you." She repeated that last formula, and a part of the street near them blew apart. Pieces of asphalt scattered in all directions. "The explosions will keep getting closer until you give me the Book, or . . ." Instead of finishing her sentence, she spoke the formula again. The blacktop just a few feet away exploded, showering them with shattered fragments of the street. "You'll be going home in pieces."

CHAPTER 23

GOING OUT WITH A BANG

Simon and Owen flinched away from the destruction. There was no way they could run—the ground around them was being torn apart, and beyond that, the street was still melted and sticky. They were trapped.

Explosions rang out closer and closer and then stopped. "No. That's not the way. I don't want to risk damaging the Book." Sirabetta sighed. "Come on, kids! I'm trying to give you a choice," she snarled. "Something *I* never had. No more games. Will you give me the Book?"

Simon and Owen, too scared to speak, shook their heads. No.

"Still you reject my kindness? Fine." Sirabetta looked

back to the formula on her leg; it resumed its glow as she gestured with both hands. The lawns nearest Owen and Simon ignited, and soon all the grass on the block was on fire. Then the street began to bubble again in earnest, causing black smoke to billow upward.

The strip of asphalt between Simon and Owen started to burn, separating the boys. They moved farther from each other and coughed at the toxic fumes coming off the street. Sirens shrieked in the distance; someone had called the police and fire departments.

Sirabetta frowned at Simon. "No help will reach you in time. Like I said, I won't risk the Book and I won't kill you, Keeper. However, I *can* destroy this little one." She pointed at Owen.

Then Owen screamed and jumped around as his sneakers burst into flame!

"No!" Simon shouted. He spoke his gravity formula, and Sirabetta braced herself for the effect.

When nothing happened, she laughed. "You're losing your touch, boy."

Simon looked on with concern as Owen stamped his feet wildly, trying to put out the flames.

Sirabetta snapped her fingers, and Owen's sneaker fires went out. "Have I made my point? Are you ready to give up?"

She shrieked as something struck her leg. It was a metal lid from one of the toppled garbage pails. "What kind of trick is this?" Sirabetta pulled off the lid and tossed it away, but it stopped several feet away in midair and spun back to her. She groaned as it smacked into her stomach. Then she turned and gulped—a manhole cover was hurtling toward her.

"What . . . what have you done?" Sirabetta asked. She quickly found a tattoo—this one silver—below the knee of her other leg. She pointed as she spoke the formula; the tattoo glowed as a softball-size ball of light flew from her outstretched hand. It whizzed at the rapidly approaching metal disk and exploded on impact, shattering the manhole cover into pebble-size pieces.

She turned back to the boys but then shrieked as the metal chunks struck her in the back. She swatted at them but couldn't brush them off—they only slid along her body. Another manhole cover scraped off the blacktop down the block and zoomed toward her. Sirabetta repeated the silver formula. The globe of light cracked the cover in two, flinging both pieces away.

Simon and Owen stared in the other direction, and Sirabetta whipped around to see various small items from the neighborhood flying through the air toward her. There were fragments of charred envelopes and jagged pieces of metal from the big mailbox, fallen trash cans (and their contents), litter from the street, and even seared toys that had been left out on one of the lawns before it burned.

Sirabetta switched legs so she could read from her heat tattoo; the oncoming paper burned to ash, the plastic melted, and the mailbox shards glowed bright red, then white, before dissolving at what must have been horrifically high temperatures.

She turned back to Simon and Owen, fists clenched, but suddenly screamed out in pain as two heavy slabs of metal— the halves of the second broken manhole cover—slammed into her. The impact knocked her over, and she fell to the ground with a clank. "What have you done to me?" she screamed in fury.

"Simon, what *did* you do to her?" Owen whispered with awe.

"Affecting her weight wasn't working, so I made *her* the center of attraction for the area's gravity. It's spreading slowly, but everything that's not bolted down—except us—is going to fall toward her as if she was the ground."

Owen laughed. "Look at her. Guess she's not so tough after all!"

Sirabetta glared at them from the ground, where she was still struggling underneath the manhole cover pieces. She used her heat formula to incinerate more small, random items flying toward her. "You think you've won?" she yelled. "This is what I get for showing mercy. I won't make that mistake again!"

She pointed toward Owen, who stared with horror as the blue heat formula on her leg glowed brightly. But they were all distracted by the sound of groaning metal. The three of them froze as Sirabetta's sleek red car flipped onto its side. It scraped toward her, quickly picking up speed as it dragged along the pavement.

"NO!" Sirabetta cried and scrambled to shift one of the manhole-cover halves—it was covering the silver tattoo she'd used. She couldn't move it enough and instead read a formula on her forearm. It glowed blue as she streaked into the air.

Simon and Owen gaped as the car changed directions; wherever Sirabetta flew, her car followed her. She soared higher, but the car just picked up speed—she was the ground to it, and the law of gravity said it had to fall to her.

Even as she fled from her car, Sirabetta shouted at the boys, "You think you're safe? You haven't stopped me! I'll never stop until that Book is mine."

"I believe her!" Owen whimpered.

Simon stared, frozen for a moment, but swiftly recovered. "We've got to get out of here," he said. "We'll have to jump like I did in the woods."

Owen nodded wildly. "Anything! Whatever it takes!"

Simon quickly lowered Owen's and his personal gravity, and they leapt over the melted street, covering hundreds of feet with their first jump. They landed far down the block and chanced a look back: Sirabetta was zigzagging through the air, trying to outrun the car. The look on her face was murderous.

Simon and Owen jumped a few more times, each leap bringing them closer to Town Plaza. "I don't know how long the gravity formula will work if I'm not there," Simon said.

They heard a distant crash and a huge explosion, followed immediately by the sound of Sirabetta shrieking, "My car!"

Simon grabbed Owen's arm to keep him from leaping again. "Change of plan; follow me." Simon shifted their gravities to be just right for reaching the roofs of the two- and three-story houses in the neighborhood. They went from rooftop to rooftop. A few people glanced out of their windows, but Simon and Owen were going so fast they probably just looked like a blur.

The boys reached Simon's house. Owen looked at Simon. "You okay?"

"I'm exhausted. Too much gravity control."

Simon's parents weren't home, so the boys went up to Simon's bedroom and called Alysha on speakerphone.

"I can't believe it! That was just a few blocks from me!" Alysha exclaimed when they told her what happened.

"Don't go outside! Ever!" Owen said.

"She's probably gone by now," Alysha said. "A bunch of fire trucks and emergency crews are out there now. My dad says it was probably a gas line rupture or something."

"No, just Sirabetta." Simon sighed wearily. "She'll never let up, will she?"

Owen took a deep breath. "At least we know two of her weaknesses."

"Two?" Alysha and Simon asked at the same time.

"Yeah," Owen said. "She can only use one formula at a time, and she can't use a formula if she can't see the tattoo."

"How do you know?" Alysha asked.

"When the manhole cover was stuck to her leg, it covered her silver tattoo; she couldn't use it to blow up her car, so she had to fly away."

Alysha whistled. "Wow. I'm impressed, Owen. Only problem is, how do we cover her other tattoos without her killing us first?"

"Hey, I can't do everything," Owen said. "I'm the scaredy-cat, remember?"

"First thing is, we've got to practice our formulas more," Simon said. "We've got to be ready next time."

They hung up after agreeing to talk more the next day and, if they felt it was safe, meet.

Owen called his mother to pick him up. He waited inside Simon's house until she got there and then sprinted for the car. As soon as he was inside, he ducked down.

"Oh, Owen." His mother shook her head. "What are you hiding from this time?"

"Trust me, you don't want to know," Owen muttered.

Once Owen was out of sight, Simon went back to his room and put the Book down on his desk. He was drained from the day's activities; just thinking the word *gravity* made him want to collapse. As he crawled into bed, he had to wonder . . . what if things got worse?

CHAPTER 24

THE ORDER GETS DISORDERLY

The next morning, I munched on a piece of toast and sipped a cup of tea; although Simon was still sleeping off his exertions from the day before, the Chronicle continued.

Back in Dunkerhook Woods, the Order of Physics had been called in for another meeting. Aside from Ralfagon, everyone who had been at the last meeting was back, including Mermon Veenie. They were all seated on their stumps, raincoat hoods tossed back, and were talking among themselves. I couldn't see Sirabetta, but she might still have been there. That baffling hooded coat of hers had managed to hide her from me in the past.

Eldonna Pombina walked over to Ralfagon's stump and

stood in front of it. She wasn't much taller than it, however, so nobody took much notice. She clapped three times.

"Attention, everyone. Please." Nobody heard her over the din of conversation. She sighed, cleared her throat, and spoke a formula. "YOUR ATTENTION, PLEASE!"

Her voice exploded across the clearing with the impact of a two-hundred-foot giant coughing into a loudspeaker. Trees swayed, leaves fell, and three hairstyles were badly messed up.

Eldonna waited until everyone pulled their hands from their ears and then reversed her formula. "Thank you," she said in her normal voice.

Willoughby Wanderby raised his hand, and Eldonna pointed to him. "Yes?"

"I believe I speak for everyone when I say, 'What?'" Willoughby shouted, his ears still ringing.

Eldonna frowned and spoke more loudly. "Sorry about the Sound Boost and any inner ear damage I may have caused. But honestly, people, this isn't a cocktail party. We're here to discuss serious matters."

"Oh, really?" Mermon Veenie growled. "Then why did our all-mighty and just leader terminate this Order's meetings in the first place? And speaking of the all-knowing man, where is he? Where is our *great* leader?"

Many faces turned and cast unfriendly glances at Veenie. Eldonna glared at Mermon and turned away from him before speaking. "Ralfagon is part of the reason I called this meeting. There's been a terrible . . . accident . . . and"—she took a deep breath—"Ralfagon Wintrofline is in the hospital."

Several members let out worried gasps and started sputtering questions, but Eldonna held up her hands to call for silence. This time, everyone hushed quickly, and she reported what she had seen at Milnes University.

The Order members were stunned, but Eldonna wasn't finished. "Campus police have called it a freak accident." Her voice turned cold. "But we know that such things are truly rare. The truck sped up to hit him, but it was driverless! And I'd swear that something prevented Ralfagon from using a formula to stop the truck. I think this was a deliberate attack!"

Confused and angry murmurs spread through the clearing. Even Veenie pretended to be upset.

"I'm sorry I didn't contact any of you," Eldonna said, beginning to sniffle, "but this is the first time I've left his side at Mountain Hospital in Stoneridge. I kept hoping he'd snap out of it. That he'd be able to tell me what to do. But now . . ." She took a deep breath. "Now I don't know. Their best doctors are watching over him. They don't know when he's going to wake up. Or even if."

Willoughby Wanderby raised his hand. "What now?" he solemnly asked when Eldonna nodded at him. "Will you guide us with the Book?"

Eldonna took another deep breath before answering. "I couldn't even if I knew how. That's the other terrible news: the *Teacher's Edition* is missing."

There was an outburst of fury and fear from the Order members.

Eldonna raised her arms, and after a few minutes, everyone quieted down again. "Please, there's still more. Someone, perhaps more than one person, entered Dunkerhook Woods after Ralfagon disbanded the Order last Sunday. I arrived early today and found some damage." Dunkerhook Woods had begun to heal itself, but the signs of the fight were still quite clear. "There are grooves in the dirt right by that chasm. And look at those bushes and that tree," she said, pointing at the stripped shrubs and the tree that had been injured by Mermon's lightning.

Myarina Myashah, a slender, dark-haired woman, spoke up. "Do you think that these intruders were Outsiders? Perhaps people from the town?"

"How?" Robertitus Charlsus replied, shaking his head. "The woods are protected from them."

Willoughby raised his hand again.

"Willoughby," Robertitus said. "We can cut the hand raising, dontchathink?"

Willoughby cleared his throat, embarrassed. "Sorry. Comes from working at a grade school. Eldonna, is it possible that someone from another Order came in and caused the damage? The formulas don't keep out other Union members."

This caused a commotion. Some shook their heads in protest; others grumbled and rubbed their chins with suspicion. The noise got louder as more members considered the possibility of another Order causing trouble.

"Perhaps we should take action," Wanderby said. "Refuse to communicate with the other Orders in the Council of Sciences. No, with every group in the Knowledge Union. Even the Board of Administration!" The Order broke into excited chatter. Wanderby continued more loudly. "Think about it, people! We can't trust anyone but ourselves. We need search parties for the Book! And security for Ralfagon. Someone has declared war on our Order; we can't just sit quietly!"

Eldonna waved her hands again, trying to restore calm. "Everyone, please. PLEASE!" she shouted. "There's no need to get hostile toward anyone yet. We don't have any suspects or clues. Besides, I was thinking we *should* seek help from the other Orders. The Biology Order has members who can heal injuries. Ralfagon always spoke of their Keeper as a friend. If they can heal Ralfagon, he might be able to tell us who attacked him or what has happened to the *Teacher's Edition*."

The members murmured as they considered this, but Wanderby slammed his doughy fist into his palm. "No! We have to be on guard against the culprits. Look around you, Eldonna! You pointed out the destruction yourself. Who else but Biology could damage Dunkerhook Woods like that? They're waiting for us to let our defenses down so they can finish Ralfagon off."

More murmurs rose among the Order.

Loisana Belane frowned. "Wait a minute . . . if they have the Book, they also have access to all our formulas."

"That's not exactly true," Eldonna said. "They'd have to figure out how to read the Book, which should be impossible. There's no need to overreact."

Mermon stood up. "No need to overreact? Look what they did to our woods! And my neighborhood!"

There was another gasp throughout the Order. Veenie nodded. "Yesterday the local police and firefighters had a real mess to deal with. The street was torn up, property was scattered, a car was blown up, and several lawns—those that gave this town its name—were set afire! The Outsiders all think it was some freak accident, but I don't believe in coincidences like that. We have enemies in the Union, and it looks like they're coming after us!"

The Order members were clearly aghast; many had heard about the explosions but had believed the Outsiders' explanation. Most forgot their long-nurtured dislike for Veenie in their need to learn more. They shouted out questions about the type of damage and if he'd seen anything.

"You see?" Wanderby said. "This is what I'm afraid of!"

"Okay, our first task is—" Eldonna started to respond.

Wanderby interrupted again; he'd apparently gotten used to skipping the hand-raising process. "We must stop them before they can master the Book! We must search out members of other Orders. They're surely roaming about as spies. We must protect our leader, our Order, and our lives!"

→ 177 ←

Order members shouted, clapped, and cheered. The ground in Dunkerhook Woods rumbled, the trees shook, and the air was filled with bursts of light and color, random weather changes, and tiny bursts of fire and electricity.

Eldonna looked on in shock as the meeting spiraled out of her control. I was equally stunned. These people, usually mild-mannered as they spent their time thinking of Physics and related matters, were acting like a bunch of soccer hooligans! I glanced at Mermon Veenie and rubbed my chin (I had an itch there). This turn of events served Veenie and Sirabetta's needs perfectly. In fact, if Veenie had suggested this, I'd have thought it was part of their plans. But Wanderby had been the one behind this chaos. And Wanderby was no friend of Veenie's and Sirabetta's . . . was he?

Flangelo, in sparrow form, observed from a nearby branch. Two things were clear to him: Mermon Veenie and Sirabetta no longer had to worry about the other Orders interfering with their plans, and Simon and his friends would find many more enemies if they got caught using their abilities.

Flangelo shifted from one leg to the other. He needed to know more about this Sirabetta before he would even consider trying to contact Gilio. He didn't want his Keeper meeting the same fate that Ralfagon had.

Still, he didn't like the thought of the children facing more trouble. He flew back to Simon's house to warn them.

CHAPTER 25

PRACTICE MAKES PERFECT

That Sunday morning, Simon waited until his parents left for their offices (they were admitted workaholics, but because it was Sunday, they waited until almost ten in the morning before heading in). He then used three-way calling to speak with Alysha and Owen at the same time and make plans for the day. Part of that plan involved going outside without getting spotted by Sirabetta or Mermon Veenie.

Simon was holding his baseball cap and a pair of sunglasses. "Alysha, are you sure about this? It's not much of a disguise."

"Trust me," Alysha said. "Famous people do the same thing all the time when they go out in public."

"Big deal," Owen said. "They're only hiding from paparazzi, not people who can blow things up by pointing at them!"

"Do you have any better ideas?" When Owen didn't answer, Alysha said, "Then just wear them."

"So where should we go?" Simon asked. "I think your neighborhood's off-limits now, Alysha."

"What neighborhood? You guys blew up most of it. Well, *she* did, anyway." Alysha paused. "The woods are probably a bad idea, right?"

"If you guys can find a way over here, my place might be good," Owen said. "It's pretty far from Alysha's; if Sirabetta is checking for us around there, we'll be safe. Plus, there's a junkyard a few blocks away. It'll be empty: it's closed on Sundays. Maybe we can practice there."

They agreed on a time, and Alysha had her father drive her over. They picked up Simon along the way. Max Davis glanced from Simon to his daughter, both wearing a cap and sunglasses. "Are we expecting reporters, kids?"

Alysha turned to Simon in the backseat. "See? I *told* you we'd look fine!"

Simon mustered a brief smile and then went back to staring out the window. Each time they passed a car or a house, he had to wonder . . . *Are they there? Are they watching for us?*

After Alysha's father dropped them off and Owen came out to meet them, Simon said, "Alysha, why don't you use your formula and start storing up random energy?"

"I did before I left home. I even drained a little electricity from my house just in case." She frowned. "I wonder what my parents' electricity bill is going to be."

The three walked down Owen's street in silence, alert for any sign of danger. Five minutes later, they arrived at the junkyard unscathed.

The gate in the chain-link fence was closed and pad-locked, but the trio climbed over easily. There were heaps of old, rusted-out metal. Pipes, tools, dishwashers, refrigerators, many other appliances, and even cars were spread out around them.

Owen spread his arms. "What do you think?"

Simon pulled off his cap and sunglasses as he looked around. "This is it."

Alysha wrinkled her nose. "This is what? Dirty? Smelly?"

"The perfect training ground." Simon let out a whoop and ran toward the nearest pile of abandoned appliances. He used friction control on his feet to glide across the dirt ground and then used his gravity command to make the nearest old washing machine weightless. He restored friction and slid to a stop in front of the washer, then reached down and grabbed hold of its sides.

He tried to lift it, but it was harder than he thought; although it weighed nothing, it still had the same mass and was thus difficult to move. He heaved and slowly raised it until he held it over his head. Once he had it up there, he felt like some sort of superhero.

"This," he shouted, "would be a great place for a battle." He started to run toward Owen and, after a few steps, threw the washing machine as if it were a huge metal soccer ball. "Owen, catch!"

It moved through the air in a straight line, going a little faster than Simon had been running. Owen closed his eyes for a second, then smiled and opened them. "Got it." He spoke his formula, and the washer stopped in midair above his head; he'd robbed it of its velocity. He concentrated and rephrased his formula, sending the washer hurtling toward a pile of car engines.

They heard a loud whirring sound as a hubcap sailed through the air like a Frisbee, only this hubcap was glowing. It struck the machine with a loud *BOOM*; the appliance was knocked out of the air before it could hit the engines. It crunched to the ground in two pieces.

Simon and Owen stared with their mouths open. They turned back to Alysha as she smacked her hands together. She saw their looks and shrugged. "What, didn't you know? Metal is a great conductor of electricity."

They played with their formulas for hours, finding new ways to use them and steadily improving their control. They also practiced fighting in reduced gravity while sliding in low friction, or while being launched by velocity. Alysha found she could drain old car or appliance batteries for energy. She even found a small generator in a toolshed and drained some of its power.

"That's *so* tingly!" Alysha said with a giggle. "I could keep a good charge going for a while with this thing." She looked around. "We should do it."

"Do what?" Simon and Owen asked.

"Use this place as a battleground," she said. "Find a way to lure Scare-a-betta and Mermon Sleazy here and take 'em down. There's a generator and spare batteries, plus all this metal for me to electrify. And there's plenty of junk for you two to throw or use as shields against attack formulas. We could really kick butt!"

Simon nodded. "Not a bad idea. And I just got another one. Book, can I handle any more formulas?"

A glowing answer appeared. "'Only one until you have more experience and stamina,'" Simon read aloud. "Okay," he said to his friends. "What do you think of this? We somehow get the bad guys here where we're hiding so we can ambush them!"

"Hiding where?" Owen asked. "It's no good to be behind a pile of junk if Sirabetta is flying overhead."

Simon grinned. "No, but what if she can't see us? Flangelo said it's easy to become invisible; what if I find a formula that keeps us out of sight?"

Owen shook his head. "Sounds like a bad idea, being invisible. What if we can't become visible again? What if we can't see ourselves? What if we're crossing the street and a car that can't see us zooms by and smacks into us?"

"Relax," Alysha said. "We could just wait here, sitting

→ 183 ←

comfortably; maybe Simon can friction–slide to lead Mr. and Ms. Evil in. And then, *bam*! You and I jump out and get them! The perfect plan!"

"Book," Simon said, "can you show me what to do to make us invisible?"

The Book answered, and Simon read it aloud again. "'There are several ways to do so, mostly through bending of light or shifting of color for camouflage. Each has its own drawbacks and advantages.'"

"Wait, Sirabetta can become invisible," Owen said. "What if she can sense when others are, too? Maybe she can see invisible things!"

"Owen, anyone ever tell you that you worry a lot?" Alysha groaned.

"Actually," Simon said, "he makes a good point."

"Fine," Alysha said. "Simon, what about that color–camouflage thing, then?"

"Book? Can you show me that?" The Book flipped to the chapter dealing with the visible spectrum. "Wow," Simon said. "There's a lot of detail here. Maybe I'll just experiment a bit."

Owen gasped. "Not again! Simon, the last time you just experimented, we almost splatted into a big hole! And before that—"

"I know, I know. But I'll test it on myself, and I'll be holding the Book. If something goes wrong, I can just reverse it." He put his finger on the symbols he planned on using. "You guys stand back. I'm going to blend in with the colors around me, like a chameleon." He scratched his head. "I think," he muttered.

Simon read the words, and there was a bright burst of light. Owen jumped back, and even Alysha flinched away.

"Did it work?" Simon asked.

Owen squinted. "I'm really not sure."

"Something happened," Alysha said. "But what?"

"Is it just me," Simon asked, "or do things look kind of funny?" He wasn't even sure if his eyes were open or not. He couldn't tell anything apart; either everything around him had disappeared, or somehow it all looked the same. "Tell me what you see."

"Everything around you is . . ." Alysha trailed off.

"Why didn't you listen to me?" Owen moaned.

"What he means is . . ." Alysha began.

"What?" Simon screamed. "Just tell me what you see!"

"*Banana!*" Owen yelled.

Simon groaned as he realized what Owen meant. Everything around him was a painfully bright shade of yellow. "I can't even see myself!" Worse, he couldn't see the Book and thus couldn't undo the formula. "Are you guys yellow, too?"

Owen and Alysha stared at the field of yellowness, like a huge blotch of paint had poured out of the sky and splattered that one spot. Owen tiptoed over to the edge of the yellowness and gingerly stuck his hand across the border. As he did so, his fingertips and then his whole hand disappeared.

His hand wasn't invisible but rather as yellow as everything around it and thus impossible to distinguish from its surroundings. He yanked his hand back, and it looked normal again. "No, we're fine unless we get too close to you."

Alysha whistled in amazement. "Try just walking out of it," she suggested.

Simon followed the sound of her voice. "Keep talking so I can—ouch!"

"Are-you-okay?" Owen hollered.

"I'm fine—I'm trying to follow your voice, but I tripped over something."

Simon slowly emerged from the field of yellow to the sound of Owen's steady chatter. Simon reversed the command, returning the junkyard to normal. Then he saw the problem.

"Oops. I guess I read it right in front of that shed." It was the same shade of blinding yellow, and he'd accidentally changed the whole area to blend in with it. "Maybe we should forget about camouflage."

Alysha and Owen murmured in agreement. Alysha leaned against a dishwasher. "Is anyone else feeling wiped out?"

Simon and Owen nodded. "It's from using your formula too much," Simon said. "Trust me, we just need food and sleep to recharge."

Alysha reached into her own book bag and took out a paper sack. "Good thing I brought snacks."

They ate sandwiches and chips in silence for a while. Owen took a swig of apple juice and cleared his throat. "You know what the problem with the junkyard plan is? Let's say we lure the bad guys and beat them. What do we do then? I'm not going to kill anybody!"

Alysha held up her hands. "Whoa, Speedy! We just have to catch them."

"I see what you mean, Owen," Simon said. "We can't exactly bring them to the police."

"No," Alysha said, "but we can turn them over to someone from the Order of Physics. They must have their own jails and stuff."

They heard a loud chirp and turned in time to see Flangelo change from bird to man behind them. "Bad idea, little spark plug. A very bad idea."

Alysha folded her arms. "Were you watching us the whole time?"

"If you're not a spy, what do you call that?" Owen demanded.

"My, aren't we confrontational," Flangelo said. "Power trip, hmm? Trust me, mini–motormouth, you're going to be glad I've been flapping those wings around town. Not only did I see your big brawl yesterday"—he clapped a few times—"but I found out some very bad news."

Flangelo told them about that morning's meeting in Dunkerhook Woods. "So you see, you do *not* want to be chatting with those Physics fellows. I promise you, they will not be warm and cuddly with you. And hiding in a patch of yellow just won't cut it."

Simon frowned. "What can we do?"

Flangelo looked away, and his voice lost its usual lilt. "I wish I could tell you. I really do. I definitely can't contact Gilio now. If he came alone, he'd probably get ambushed by the Physics members. If he came with the rest of the Order of Biology, it would lead to a war. Frankly, I'm terrified just flapping around. If they recognize me as a Bio member, they might tear me apart."

Owen, distressed, spoke extra quickly. "That-woman-Eldonna-if-we-talk-to-her-she'll-make-things-okay-with-the-others!"

Flangelo just stood and stared for a moment. "I'd swear that was English in fast-forward. Isn't there a medication for him?"

"Leave him alone," Alysha said with a frown. "He's right. We should explain things to this Eldonna. She might help us."

Flangelo shrugged. "That could work. She seemed pretty rough, with her megaphone trick, but you never know. She's probably at the hospital."

"Then let's go," Simon said. "Once she knows it's not Biology's fault, you'll be safe, too."

Flangelo shook his head. "I wouldn't go now. The Order members might be visiting or keeping guard. Your best bet is tomorrow, when they're at work."

Owen's jaw dropped. "The Order members have jobs?"

Flangelo twitter-laughed. "Of course. How much money do you think there is in stomping around magic woods? They've got bills to pay, right? Union members generally stick to educational-type jobs; it goes with their whole help-humanity-progress motif." He saw their blank looks. "Motif. Theme. Never mind."

"So tomorrow we skip school and go to the hospital," Simon said.

"No way," Owen said. "My mom would kill me!"

"Yeah, same here," Alysha said. "I do *not* want to get grounded."

"I can go alone," Simon said.

"No way!" Owen said. "We're a team, and we stick together." Alysha nodded in agreement.

Simon sighed. "Fine. After school, it's straight to the hospital. And if we run into Veenie or Sirabetta, we try to lure them here."

"Or anywhere with lots of stuff to throw and electricity to drain," Owen said.

Alysha clapped Owen and then Simon on the back. "Which is basically everywhere in town. Boys, we are ready!"

Flangelo was quiet as he watched them leave the junkyard. He didn't look as confident as they were; in fact, he looked very worried for them.

I felt the same way.

CHAPTER 26

A Time and a Space for Everything

Simon got home from the junkyard; though worn out from the long day of practicing, he was exhilarated, too. He walked into his bedroom, tossed the Book on his desk, and sat down on his bed. A good meal, a good night's sleep, and he'd be ready for anything.

There was a knock at his door. "Come in."

Sylvia Bloom entered. "Ah, you're home! You've been out all day."

"Yeah, I was off with some friends. Um, science work."

Sylvia smiled. "My boys and their science. Your father's downstairs in his office, plugging away. I'm glad you're safe, especially after what I heard."

Simon gulped. "What did you hear, Mom?"

"Some disaster on the other side of Town Plaza yesterday evening; not too far from here, you know. They're saying it was some ruptured pipes, but I saw photos in a newspaper at the office; that street was a mess. It made me wonder about you, off on your own all day. Are you being careful?"

"Oh yeah. Taking every precaution."

Sylvia rubbed his hair affectionately. "Good. It can be a dangerous world, you know. Terrible, terrible accidents." She sighed and then brightened. "Okay, I've got some more work to do. Thai takeout for dinner?"

"Yeah," Simon said. "I'm starving." But she was already out the door. Simon looked over at the Book and frowned. That fight with Sirabetta had been so destructive. So dangerous. He and his friends would probably have to face her again. They'd have to win this time; they couldn't keep running. Would all their practice today be enough? Or would he need an extra edge after all?

Simon searched his room for anything that could be useful in a fight. He stuffed a few items into his backpack, including a paintball gun he'd gotten on his last birthday. I nodded in appreciation, realizing Simon's plan; even if it didn't work, those things really sting when they hit.

Still, Simon suspected he'd need something more. "Book, I need your help."

The Book's clasp popped open, and the cover rose a few inches, waiting for its Keeper's request.

"I want to use a third formula, but not camouflage. I need something that might let me beat Sirabetta, something that can get past her tricks. Do you have anything that can do that?"

The Book responded in writing. *Possibly—but it could be dangerous.*

Simon thought of the terrible formulas Sirabetta had at her disposal. "I understand. I'll take that risk." The Book turned to a new chapter, and Simon gasped at what he saw.

He read the text but found it hard to follow. He wished he could just look at Alysha's *Physics for the Doofus* book, but he didn't want Alysha or Owen to know he was learning a third formula. Not until he understood how to use it.

After a few minutes of clueless reading, Simon muttered, "I told Mom I'd be careful; maybe I should be." He went downstairs and approached the closed door of his father's home office, a cluttered room down the hall from the recreation room. He knocked gently. "Dad? Can I come in?"

There was the sound of shuffling papers and then a voice said, "It's open."

Simon entered and looked around at the shelves crammed with hundreds of serious-looking books and a desk cluttered with more books and folders.

Steven reached over and clicked off his computer monitor, but not before Simon noticed a series of strange graphs on the screen.

"I need to ask you something," Simon said. "It's kind of important. Urgent." He added, "For school."

Steven tugged on an ear and bit his lip. "I guess I can spare a few minutes."

"It's for science class. About space–time and relativity."

Steven's mouth dropped open. "In sixth grade? School has gotten more advanced since my day." He scratched his frizzy hair. "Okay, what, specifically?"

"Uh, what are space–time and relativity? How do they work? Basically?"

Steven chuckled. "Oh, I was worried you had a tough question." He cleared his throat. "Sir Isaac Newton said that everyone and everything moves through four dimensions. There are three physical dimensions—length, width, and depth—and a fourth dimension: time. We're all moving forward in time. If I wanted to describe the exact location of, say, us, I'd have to use the coordinates of *where* we are and *when* we are. But Einstein came up with the space–time continuum, which describes all four dimensions together in one system that exists all around us. He said the where and when depend on the observer; time and space aren't universal."

Simon blinked a few times while trying to process that. "Okay."

Steven went on. "Einstein had a special and a general theory of relativity. Both deal with space–time. The general theory talks about curved space–time, gravity, and the possibility of black holes. And I'm sure you've heard of the special theory's famous formula, $E = mc^2$? The relationship between energy, mass, and the speed of light?"

Simon shook his head slowly.

Steven chewed his lower lip. "What *exactly* do you want to know?"

Simon shrugged. "Maybe practical applications of space–time?"

Steven looked astonished. "Practical? Sorry, pal, they're only theories, for use in figuring out how the universe works."

"I mean, like in the science–fiction stuff I read . . ."

Steven frowned. "Oh, Simon, that stuff is trash. Pure nonsense. Pseudofuturistic daydreams. Not to mention all that silly manipulating of the laws of physics however the authors want to, paying no heed to the real world."

Simon tried hard not to smile; if his father only knew! "How would space–time work if someone *could* use it?"

Steven ran a hand through his frizzy hair. "Let's see. If you could somehow travel through space–time on Earth, you could instantly go from one place to another in time and/or space. Teleportation or wormholes would be possible, I suppose, because controlling space–time is controlling *where* and *when* something is, right? Maybe mastery of space–time could even let you change the flow of time entirely. Perhaps slow time down, speed it up, even reverse it."

Simon felt even wearier now than before. "Got it. Thanks, Dad."

"I am impressed that you've taken such an interest in science." Steven seemed to quietly struggle with something, then took a deep breath and asked, "Do you want to see something interesting?"

Simon nodded.

"Now, Simon, you have to promise not to tell anybody. Not your mother, not your friends."

Simon nodded again, surprised. "I swear."

"Then let's go to the basement."

Steven took a set of keys from his desk and one of the folders from the desktop, and then he led Simon into the basement. He stopped at the file cabinet with padlocks on the drawers and unlocked and opened the second drawer from the top. "I've been looking into something . . . odd."

He pulled out a folder of photos, notes, and graphs. "There have been strange readings in this town for as long as there's been a science department at Milnes. Barometric pressure, seismic activity, electrical energy, and more. I usually deal with astrophysics, but lately, I've been looking into reports of local disturbances, too. For example, yesterday's alleged gas main problem, or whatever the papers called it? My instruments at the lab picked up some unique readings. And there've been fascinating eyewitness reports; a handful of townspeople claimed they saw someone—or something— fly past their houses yesterday."

I gasped as Steven Bloom pulled out a photo of a man I recognized well. A stooped, gray-haired man, wearing a faded overcoat and holding his cane: Ralfagon Wintrofline. Although Simon didn't recognize him, he felt the Book vibrating gently inside his book bag.

"This man is a physics professor at Milnes University," Steven said. "His name is Ralph Winter, but once when we were speaking, he referred to himself as 'Ralfagon.' A very odd man. Some say he's just scatterbrained, some say he's insane. All agree he's brilliant. I've met with him several times to discuss my theories about this town. I think . . . I may be on track for major breakthroughs in the field of physics."

Simon struggled to keep his brain from jumping out and doing a somersault. His father knew Ralfagon! His father was researching activities of the Order of Physics! And his father's instruments had picked up on Simon and Owen's fight with Sirabetta!

Steven continued. "I plan on checking in with Professor Winter to get his opinion on this latest incident." He checked his watch and frowned. "In fact, I'd better get back to work now. You won't say anything about our chat, right, pal?"

"Top secret, Dad. And thanks for your help."

Steven smiled. "Glad to see you so caught up in science."

Simon coughed as he walked out. "Oh, yeah. Big fan."

CHAPTER 27

CHOSEN SIDES

On Monday morning, I watched Alysha come to school. As soon as her father dropped her off in front, she walked by the packs of students over to Rachelle at the front steps.

"Hey, how was your weekend?" Alysha asked.

Rachelle looked at her and sniffed. "Fine. I was with my *real* friends." She made a show of looking at her watch. "Oh, I've got to go." Rachelle turned her back on Alysha and joined the rest of her clique on the other side of the stairway.

Alysha thought of demanding to know what was going on. Then she noticed Marcus, Barry, and some other guys standing near the girls. All were glaring at her.

She went up the steps into the school, trying to ignore what had just happened.

Alysha was startled to find Miss Fanstrom waiting just inside the entrance, her ever-present briefcase in one hand. The principal's hair didn't move an inch as she nodded to Alysha. "Well done, Miss Davis. Stiff upper lip, stay strong."

"Miss—Miss Fanstrom?" Alysha stammered. "Uh, thanks."

"You're doing fine, dear," Miss Fanstrom said. She patted her briefcase, making a quiet *thunk* sound against the notebook computer inside. "You all are." Then she turned and walked off without waiting for a response. Alysha saw the top of the tower of hair point at her and then swivel to face down the hall. She looked in that direction and saw Simon and Owen walking toward her with big grins.

Alysha wasn't sure what to think of Miss Fanstrom's words or hair, but she didn't have much spare energy that day. She had slept a lot the night before and had eaten a huge dinner and breakfast, so she didn't think her weariness was from using her new formula.

Still, she had to struggle to pay attention; it didn't help that every class included at least one person from her clique. And none of them were talking to her.

Lunch was the hardest. She was used to finding at least Rachelle, if not several other girls, too, waiting at her locker to walk with her to the lunchroom. Today, she was on her own. She joined the back of the food line and saw none of her group among the waiting students. Maybe they'd walked over to Nezzo's and had forgotten to tell her? No, she didn't believe that.

She found the truth quickly when she exited the food line and entered the main cafeteria. The cavernous room was filled with its usual din of the laughing, singing (mostly from the younger grades), and chattering of grades one through six, spread across dozens of long, drab-gray Formica tables. She gazed across the bustling room and saw the table the popular kids always sat at, nestled in the back far from the crowded entrance, food line, and garbage pails. The table was full.

Everyone was there, eating and gabbing and joking and smiling. Everyone was having a great time . . . without her. Alysha stood staring, holding her cafeteria tray loaded with food, and locked eyes with Rachelle. Rachelle said something that made the whole table turn to stare at her. To frown at her. Why? What had she done? She decided to ask them: maybe it was some dumb misunderstanding.

She moved quickly past all the other tables and headed to her usual spot on the popular table's bench. As she neared, though, her friends made a point of spreading out so there wasn't room for her. "Table's full," Barry said.

Rachelle scowled. "Why don't you go sit with your loser buddies?"

"What?"

"We saw you," Rachelle said. "We *all* saw you! On Saturday. Outside Nezzo's. With *them*. Marcus saw you holding hands with that puke boy, Simon."

"I wasn't holding hands—wait, what did you call him?" Alysha demanded.

Rachelle spun around and flicked her hand in the air behind her, as if flinging Alysha away.

Alysha ground her teeth and for a moment thought of yelling at Rachelle. Yelling at them all. She felt a surge of energy, as if she'd just downed a full can of soda; then she noticed the lights in the cafeteria were flickering. She gasped, looking from the lights above to the nearest outlet, just a few feet away on the wall. Sparks of electricity were leaping across the distance into her legs. She'd activated her formula without even realizing it, and now she was draining from the school!

She turned and walked out of the cafeteria, tray in hand, and hurried out to the playground. She stepped carefully around the younger kids and found Simon and Owen seated inside one of those concrete tubes.

"We weren't sure what you were going to do for lunch," Simon said, "so we figured we'd just go to our usual spot."

Alysha frowned. "We've got trouble. Well, I do, and you two probably will. Marcus saw us in front of Nezzo's, and it looks like he—no, all of those guys—are pretty angry. You two should watch your step around them: they can get kind of nasty."

Owen shook his head. "Maybe he should watch his step around us! We don't have to take it anymore, do we? I'd like to give him a taste of increased velocity!"

Alysha raised her eyebrows. "Wow. Bravery *and* breathing between words."

Simon sighed. "Owen, I don't think slamming the school jerk with your formula is going to help. Flangelo said we should keep a low profile, right?"

Owen's words started speeding up. "Yeah–but–that–doesn't–mean–we–should–just–sit–around–and–let–Marcus–and–Barry–pummel–us!"

"Why don't we see if we can just avoid them for now?" Simon said. "They haven't said a word to me all day."

Owen shrugged. "Me neither."

"Same here," Alysha said. "But we've got the last class of the day with them." She nodded as Simon and Owen's faces tightened. "Gym class."

The rest of the day passed smoothly enough. But every class, each stop at the water fountain in the halls, and every trip past a former friend's locker while heading to her next period brought more dirty looks. This all annoyed Alysha, but she managed to keep her anger under control. As she came out of the girls' locker room for her last class, she saw the gym teacher sitting in the bleachers. His name was

Willoughby Wanderby—the very same Willoughby Wanderby from the Order of Physics (unlike most Union members, he hadn't changed his name on entering . . . with a name like that, there was no need).

Wanderby was preoccupied with a detailed folding map of Lawnville, using fluorescent green Post-it notes to mark certain spots. Then he periodically made a quiet but anxious call on his cell phone. Just as the waiting students were starting to get truly restless, Mr. Wanderby snapped his phone shut and refolded the map. Standing up, he blew a short blast on his whistle. "Okay, lads, lasses . . . dodgeball!"

A hush fell across the students in the gymnasium. Dodgeball was the most awful or exhilarating game in gym, depending, of course, on how good you were at it. Many schools had banned it for its brutality.

Mr. Wanderby looked around and zeroed in on Marcus. For some reason, Marcus was the only student he ever called by name (and always by his last name). "Van Ny, captain. And . . ." Wanderby searched the faces for the rival captain.

Alysha watched Wanderby as he tried to make up his mind for the second captain. He squinted at her (she had been chosen twice before), and then his gaze lingered on Owen, who was sitting next to her. That was strange. Wanderby usually only paid attention to Owen when he was hurt (not rare) or making a fuss (quite often).

Then Wanderby looked at Simon. This was new. Mr. Wanderby, like most other teachers, generally treated Simon as if he were invisible. But today, Wanderby's gaze landed on Simon and didn't leave. In fact, he stared.

He leaned forward for an even closer look, then shook his head, as if dismissing a crazy thought. He pointed at Simon. "You, lad. You're captain, too," he said, ignoring the startled whispers.

Simon picked Owen and Alysha right away and then randomly chose the rest; he didn't care who else was with them. When the whistle blew, Marcus and Barry grabbed rubber balls and immediately nailed two students near Simon.

The boy Barry hit collapsed to one knee and gasped for air as he held his stomach. The boy Marcus hit lay flat for a few moments before he crawled away and curled up into a ball.

Barry and Marcus quickly scooped up another rubber ball each; Marcus glanced at Wanderby, who was studying the map again and was clearly too absorbed to pay attention to the game. Then Marcus pointed at Simon, Owen, and Alysha from across the gym and drew his free hand across his throat. "Who wants to die first?" he bellowed.

Alysha flinched as someone else on her team went down from a viciously thrown ball. So much for the day ending smoothly.

CHAPTER 28

A Sweet Yet Bitter Victory

The gymnasium was filled with dodgeball chaos. Rubber balls flew back and forth, causing groans and, occasionally, screams with every *boing* of impact.

Simon looked around at his team. It was a massacre. Marcus and Barry were the undisputed champs of dodgeball, after all. He saw the fear in Owen's eyes as Marcus threw a ball that whizzed right past his face. His face! If that had hit Owen, it could have broken his nose!

"Marcus, what is your problem?" Alysha screamed.

Marcus sneered. "Ask your new boyfriends, the loser twins!" He grabbed another ball and hurled it. Alysha ducked. Barely. Marcus was out for blood. "This stops here. Now," Simon said.

Owen looked over at Simon. "What–did–you–say–what–are–you–doing–grab–that–ball–oh–no–they're–going to–kill–us–they're–going to–kill–me!"

Owen dove out of the way of the latest throw. As Owen rose shakily to his feet, Simon made a decision.

There were only a couple of kids still standing on their team besides Owen, Alysha, and him. Marcus and Barry had probably told their teammates to save the three friends for last. A quiet, chubby girl was one of the other two remaining teammates. She ran screaming near Simon as she narrowly dodged a ball. The next throw, hurled by Barry, streaked toward her head. But Simon got there first.

He grabbed a rubber ball from the floor and quickly threw it at the incoming one. He whispered his gravity formula so his ball was drawn to Barry's, as if Barry's ball was the ground and Simon's ball was falling sideways toward it. Then Simon increased the gravitational pull many times; the ball flew as if he'd thrown it extremely fast.

Simon's ball knocked into Barry's a foot away from the terrified girl's face, saving her from a painful hit. Simon canceled the gravity attraction just as they collided (otherwise the balls would have stuck together). A gasp went up from everyone in class, and Barry snarled. He looked at Marcus, who nodded. Barry grabbed another loose ball and hurled it at Simon's head with intent to pummel.

Simon again used his gravity control, reducing the weight of Barry's ball so the ball drifted higher than aimed. He also lessened the friction on his own feet. The other kids probably thought Simon was the luckiest kid in the world when he dodged the throw. Owen and Alysha knew the truth, though, and their jaws dropped.

In that moment, the girl Simon had saved and the other remaining player, a tall, skinny boy, were eliminated. That left Simon, Alysha, and Owen against Marcus, Barry, and six others. Eight against three: tough dodgeball odds anywhere, but with Marcus and Barry against them, it should have been impossible.

Simon locked eyes with Alysha and Owen. He nodded slowly and with meaning. They returned the gesture . . . they were ready.

Alysha and Simon both grabbed loose balls. Owen whispered his formula and nodded to Alysha. She had good aim and, with Owen's velocity boost, her ball whizzed across the gym and nailed one of the boys. Simon used his friction to help her slip under a throw from Marcus. Then Simon shifted gravity so the next ball he threw zoomed and hit another boy's leg.

A girl on Marcus's team threw her ball at Simon, but Simon curved it, using gravity, and grabbed it, using friction (it literally stuck to his hands). Several students gasped at this, but it was Owen who caused the most stir.

Barry threw a ball with bone–cracking speed; it should have smashed Owen in the ribs. Instead, Owen canceled its velocity so the ball stopped just as Owen wrapped his arms around it. As far as anyone in the class knew, Owen had just caught a ball thrown by Barry. Barry was out!

Everyone gasped. Then those on Simon's team got over their shock and cheered.

The noise alerted Mr. Wanderby, who looked up from his research. Simon saw the shocked expression on the teacher's face and smiled. Mr. Wanderby would never forget this day: the day Marcus and Barry fell.

Alysha, Simon, and Owen got the last three members of Marcus's team out. That left Simon, Owen, and Alysha against Marcus.

Marcus grabbed a ball. "I'm going to pound all three of you!" he snarled.

Owen, having grabbed a new ball, cocked back his arm. "Hey, Marcus, how does it feel to be losing to losers?"

The whole class fell silent: a nobody like Owen had dared to taunt Marcus.

Marcus threw first, but Owen used velocity, and his rubber ball rocketed across the room. It struck at the per–fect angle, sending Marcus's own rubber ball streaking back into his face. He was out! Marcus's team had lost, and his nose was bleeding all over his gleaming white gym T-shirt.

Simon's team erupted in applause and cheers. They had just witnessed the impossible. Even some members of Marcus's team clapped; in the past they, too, had suffered welts and bruises from playing against Marcus and Barry.

Mr. Wanderby did not look excited. In fact, he glared at Owen, Alysha, and Simon. For a long moment, the students watched him and waited for some reaction. After all, the game had just ended.

Finally, Mr. Wanderby walked over to Marcus and checked the boy's nose. "Van Ny, do you want to go to the nurse?"

Marcus stared evilly at Owen, Simon, and Alysha. "No. I want to play again."

Wanderby shifted his angry stare over to Simon and his friends. "Well done. Play again," he said through gritted teeth.

Only this time, Mr. Wanderby never looked down at his map. As Simon, Alysha, and Owen used their formulas to lead the team to a crushing victory over Marcus's (with Barry and Marcus both receiving painful hits this time), Mr. Wanderby watched every move. He glowered the whole time.

I WAS WORRIED THIS WOULD HAPPEN

I was pleased to see how well Simon, Owen, and Alysha did; I'm no fan of bullies. Simon's team won so easily that there was time for four games total. By the end of the second game, every student seemed to realize that Simon, Owen, and Alysha were unstoppable.

By the end of the third game, Barry had developed a limp and Marcus had one eye swollen shut. By the end of the fourth, they were bloody and badly bruised. Wanderby didn't look at them; he only had eyes for Simon, Owen, and Alysha.

When the bell rang, Wanderby dismissed the class. "Except for you three. Our heroes. Why don't you get changed, get your books and such, and meet me back in the gym?"

Alysha, Owen, and Simon nodded; why not? They'd just caused the greatest upset in Martin Van Buren Elementary's dodgeball history!

Marcus and Barry hobbled off to the locker room. Barry swore off playing ever again; for days after, he was heard whispering that he could still hear the balls bouncing.

As for Marcus, he was convinced that Simon, Alysha, and Owen were working some terrible magic on him. He shambled to the nurse's office to have his many injuries looked at; he'd have his father pick him up later.

In the boys' locker room, Owen and Simon received congratulations from everyone else. For the first time in their lives, Simon and Owen knew what it felt like to be embraced by their classmates. Alysha also welcomed the cheers the girls gave her in the locker room. After a day of being snubbed by her old friends, she was glad to have other classmates be nice to her.

After getting changed, Simon, Alysha, and Owen went to their lockers and walked back to the gym together. Simon and Owen were feeling weary again, but they weren't worried. In just a few minutes, they would leave the school, find Eldonna, and explain the Book situation. As far as they knew, their problems were nearly solved.

Mr. Wanderby came out of his office. "Good, you're here." His voice was especially harsh. "I won't mince words. I know one of you has the Book, so let's have it back before things get worse."

Simon, Alysha, and Owen stared blankly. Could Mr. Wanderby possibly mean the *Teacher's Edition*? Could he know about the Knowledge Union?

Wanderby sneered. "Playing dumb, are you?" He spoke a formula and gestured to a garbage can in the corner of the gym. They watched in bewilderment as it spun faster and faster, rotating in place until the lid went flying and trash spewed all over the polished floor.

Wanderby glared. "That was a warning. Next time, it'll be your heads."

CHAPTER 29

THINGS GET REALLY HAIRY

Owen stared at the wrecked garbage can. "But we won at dodgeball!" he sputtered.

"Owen, he must be in the Order," Alysha said. "Mr. Wanderby, let us explain!"

"Oh, I'm sure I know enough. Give me the *Teacher's Edition*."

"Let's skate out of here," Simon said. "We'll talk to Eldonna, and she'll clear things up with him later." He spoke the words for friction, and the three friends slid for the exit.

Wanderby gestured, reactivating his formula. The kids stopped sliding forward and instead started to spin. It was slow at first.

"I do not like having to repeat myself. Lass, lads, I want that Book!"

Wanderby spoke a few new words. Simon, Alysha, and Owen spun in place, going faster and faster; the lack of friction on their feet made Wanderby's formula especially effective. The world soon became a blur as they whipped around.

Finally, they slowed down and the world came back into focus. They collapsed to the ground, and though they'd stopped spinning, everything seemed to keep whirling.

Wanderby walked over to them and folded his arms across his chest. "Which of you has it? Come now, cooperate or I'll start again. If your heads pop off, the blood will make an awful mess."

A commanding English accent echoed within the gym. "Mr. Wanderby, explain yourself!" Simon, Alysha, and Owen strained to look around the room and see who had spoken. It was Miss Fanstrom!

She took long strides across the floor, swinging her arms angrily.

Wanderby was stunned. "Miss Fanstrom? This does not concern you."

Miss Fanstrom shook her head, her gigantic column of black hair remaining still. "Oh, I disagree. I am the principal, not you. In this school, the principal is responsible for discipline. And I certainly do not approve of your methods." She pointed to the spilled garbage can. "It's bad enough you can't remember the children's names, but to spread trash like that?" Then she gestured to the kids. "And there is *no* spinning in school."

Wanderby frowned. "Please leave us alone. These are matters that you could not possibly understand."

Miss Fanstrom stepped up to Wanderby and looked down to meet his gaze. (She was several inches taller, not even counting her hair.) "I understand far more than you think. Far more than *you* understand." Her voice was clipped and stern.

"You leave me no choice," Wanderby said. He started to speak his formula, but then Miss Fanstrom's hair went into motion.

The tower of hair stretched forward like the extremely thick tentacle of a shaggy octopus. It smacked Wanderby across the face, cutting him off before he could get halfway through his formula. Then the hair rose up above him and banged down on his head like a gigantic, fuzzy hammer.

Willoughby Wanderby sank to the floor, unconscious.

Miss Fanstrom walked over to the kids and clucked her tongue. "Tut, tut, children. If you were using your heads, you would have found a way to counteract Mr. Wanderby's formula. He was only controlling rotational motion."

The three friends lay staring, unable to respond. A few seconds later, Owen leaned over and threw up.

Miss Fanstrom sighed. "Mr. Walters, that is not a proper answer."

She tapped a button on a remote control attached to her

belt, and the kids' dizziness stopped immediately. She had canceled out the effects of Wanderby's formula! She winked at them. "A little gizmo a friend gave me long ago. Comes in handy." She waited a moment. "Very well, up you go. This is no time to rest. Miles to go before you sleep, so to speak."

Simon, Alysha, and Owen slowly rose to their feet. Although the dizziness was gone, Simon and Owen were still a bit drained from using their formulas so much.

Miss Fanstrom gave Owen a breath mint, which he popped in his mouth and chewed. "Well done earlier, by the way. Since I arrived I've felt that Mr. Van Ny and Mr. Stern could use a good drubbing."

She turned and headed for the gym's exit. After a moment, she turned back to the three friends. "Are you coming or not? I do have other matters to attend to, you know. I'd hate for Mr. Wanderby to wake up while we're standing here; I don't want to use more-drastic measures on him. Other things aside, he's a very good gym teacher."

They walked with Miss Fanstrom, too numb to ask any questions. She pulled out a small yellow pad and scribbled a number onto a sheet of paper. She handed the sheet to Simon. "Here. This is the apartment you want. See the man who lives there and he'll give you a bit of information. Not too much, I imagine, but just enough to get you through this. Frankly, he could use the company."

Simon cleared his throat. "Get us through what, Miss Fanstrom?"

Miss Fanstrom smiled. "Ah, already asking questions. Very resilient. That's good. You'll need the questions and the resilience. Miles to go, miles to go."

She herded them toward her office. "I must say, I'm quite proud of you all so far," Miss Fanstrom said. "You've handled yourselves admirably. Quite. But you'll have to start reacting more quickly than you did with Mr. Wanderby. Villains don't always chatter before striking or start their attacks so slowly. If you let every surprise freeze you, you'll never make it through. Use your heads and act with confidence."

Miss Fanstrom opened the door to her office, and they followed her inside. She shut the door behind them, stepped behind her desk, and placed her notebook computer on it. She pointed to the sheet of paper in Simon's hand. "Do you understand what you're to do?"

Simon glanced down at the paper, over to Alysha and Owen, then back to Miss Fanstrom. "No."

"Good," Miss Fanstrom said dryly. "Wouldn't do for me to give you the answers. Wouldn't be much of an adventure." She opened her notebook computer and tapped at its keyboard. It beeped, and there was an answering beep from the mechanical box above the door. "Be smart and be brave. I have faith in you."

Surprisingly, Owen had the nerve to ask, "Miss Fanstrom? Is your hair alive?"

Miss Fanstrom arched an eyebrow. "Why, Mr. Walters . . . how bold." She winked and gripped the sides of her tower of hair. She wriggled her fingers into the base of the hair and lifted; the entire column rose off her head, revealing a mechanism at the bottom. It was a machine!

Underneath, Miss Fanstrom had perfectly normal hair, though it was cut very short. She winked. "Yet another useful device for someone in my position."

"Your position?" Simon asked.

Miss Fanstrom replaced her mechanical hair. "Yes. Principal." She pointed to the door. "The exit is that way. Off you go."

Simon, Alysha, and Owen nodded, a little uncertainly. They opened Miss Fanstrom's office door and behind it saw an unfamiliar corridor with dull gray-and-black carpeting, off-white walls, and several brass-fixture lamps mounted along it. It definitely wasn't part of the school. It looked more like the hallway in an apartment building.

They stepped past the doorway and turned back to look at Miss Fanstrom. She waved her hand forward. "Go on. Ahead on the right."

Still confused, Simon led Alysha and Owen down the hall. Miss Fanstrom's door shut on its own, and when the kids turned to look, it had vanished.

Simon took a deep breath and rechecked the paper in his hand. "This is it. Number one-oh-six." He knocked on the door in front of him. Nothing happened, so he knocked harder. There was the sound of locks being undone, and then the door swung open.

Simon, Alysha, and Owen looked up at a tall man who stared back at them. He was older, but they couldn't tell by exactly how much. He had dark brown hair with many strands of white throughout, a pair of thin spectacles pushed forward on his nose, and faint lines on his face. He could have been thirty or three hundred.

From the brown bathrobe he wore over striped flannel pajamas and the thick-soled slippers he had on his feet, it was clear he wasn't expecting any company.

And from the way his bespectacled eyes bugged out and his thin-lipped mouth froze in an O shape, it was clear he was shocked to see them.

The man opened and closed his mouth several times, but no words came out.

"Hello?" Alysha finally asked. "Are you alive?"

At last the man found his voice, speaking in a clear, crisp English accent. "What on Earth are you doing here?" He frowned and mumbled, "I knew that hallway looked familiar."

"We don't even know where here is," Simon said. "Who are you?"

"Why, I'm your Narrator," he said without thinking. Then he gasped and clapped a hand over his mouth. "Oh, goodness. I'm going to get into so much trouble for this!"

CHAPTER 30

THIS ISN'T SUPPOSED TO HAPPEN!

I pulled my hand away from my mouth and closed my eyes, holding them shut for a long moment. I thought I might discover I was imagining it. Alas, no: when I opened my eyes, the children were still there. Simon Bloom, Alysha Davis, and Owen Walters were standing outside *my* doorway!

"What do you mean, you're our Narrator?" Alysha demanded.

I cleared my throat. "Er, I meant to say navigator. Yes. And the direction you want is that way." I pointed to the exit while quickly closing the door. But not quickly enough—something was jammed in the doorway.

"Ouch! That's my foot!" Owen shouted.

I swung the door back open. "Terribly sorry, but you did place it in the way; I don't know why you've chosen this moment to become so courageous." Instantly, I realized my mistake and again clapped my hand to my mouth.

Alysha put her hands on her hips. "Now what the heck does that mean? Who are—?" She paused and turned back to her friends. "Do you guys hear that? That sounds like *my* voice."

I coughed loudly to cover the noise, but of course, the sound of my cough echoed from my apartment. "That's nothing. A television program I'm watching. Please leave now; I'm stricken with plague, you see, and can't have visitors."

Owen shook his head. "No, I definitely heard Alysha's voice and then his and now . . . now I hear mine."

Simon glared at me. "What's going on?"

Alysha simply pushed past me and stepped into my apartment.

"Wait a moment!" I said. "You, there, this is not how things are done!"

But it was too late. Simon and Owen followed Alysha into my apartment and all three murmured, "Whoa!" at what they saw. I put my face in my hands and groaned. This kind of thing was not supposed to happen.

Simon, Alysha, and Owen gaped at the sight of my wall-size Viewing Screen showing images of them. And me. Standing in my apartment as it was happening.

Simon and Alysha whirled to face me, both of them thinking horrible thoughts about spies or Peeping Toms. I had raised my hands, ready to protest my innocence, when I noticed Owen getting closer to the screen.

"You guys! Why didn't you tell me I had some puke on my shirt? That's disgusting!" Then he remembered what he was looking at and whipped around to face me, too. "And what's the big idea having us on your TV screen?"

Simon looked back and forth from me to the screen and then gazed around the room. He was making exactly the right conclusion, which was exactly the worst news for me. "Wait a minute! How is this working? That image . . . What kind of camera angle do you have here? Because it's impossible!" He kept turning and moving around while peeking over his shoulder to note that, sure enough, the Viewing Screen was capturing it. "No matter where I move, it's focused on me and still showing all of you. How many cameras do you have running?"

"Oh, dear," I groaned. "I'll be sacked for this, you know." The three of them had no idea what I meant. "Fired. I shall be fired. This is against procedure."

Alysha balled her hands into fists and spoke her formula, dimming the lights for a moment as she began absorbing electricity. "Have you been following us?"

"Young lady, I have not left my apartment in"—I checked my watch—"nine years, five months, ten days, and fourteen minutes. They've even changed the wallpaper in the halls since I've last been out there. And mind you, that outing was only for a building–wide fire drill." I frowned. "It was raining, too. You'd think my one time out would at least include some bloody sunshine."

"How can sunshine be bloody?" Owen asked.

I sighed. "Oh, Owen, sometimes you don't stop to think, do you? I'm English; 'bloody' is just an expression we use."

"So we're in England now?" Simon asked.

I shook my head. "No, we're still in Lawnville; I'm stationed here." I smoothed my bathrobe lapels. "But all the best Narrators are from Great Britain."

"Narrators," Simon said. "You said that before. What are you talking about?"

I shook my head again. "No. I've said too much already. Please leave."

Alysha folded her arms. "Tell us. If you've really been watching us, you know how dangerous we can be. You wouldn't like us when we're angry."

I groaned. "Very well, just stop stealing lines from *The Incredible Hulk*. I don't want my Chronicle to be accused of plagiarism."

Simon gestured with his hand. "Your Chronicle?"

"Ohmigosh, look!" Owen was the first to look at something other than the Viewing Screen or myself. To my dismay, he had found the Recording Monitor.

"What's a Recording Monitor? Why capitalize that and Viewing Screen?"

And, to my greater dismay, he was reading along. Perfect. Perhaps it was better when he just hid from everything.

Owen, of course, read this. "Hey–what–does–that–mean– what–are–you–trying–to–say—" He stared and frowned. "Do I really talk like that?"

I pointed to Alysha. "She doesn't call you Speedy for nothing, you know."

"You were about to explain," Simon said.

I rubbed at my nose beneath my eyeglasses. "Yes, fine. Only please, Owen, step away from the Monitor. The one thing more distressing than your presence here is having you read along as the tale unfolds." I spread my hands, indicating the rest of my apartment. "You might as well make yourselves comfortable. This may be a bit shocking."

The kids looked around at my three-seater sofa, polished-wood coffee table with many magazines and newspapers on it, and several fake plants (fake plants make little mess, you see).

I gestured to the couch. "Please, sit. It's about time someone used it. The problem with all your friends being Narrators is they never come over to visit—we stay home working all the time."

As they moved to the couch, Alysha decided to be nice, probably to soften me up a bit. "You've kept it very neat."

I smiled. "Of course. I'm English," I said before going into the kitchen. "First let me get you some food and drink; after all that formula use, you'll need to eat a lot. How about left-over Nezzo's? It's from yesterday, so it's still fresh enough."

"You order from Nezzo's?" Alysha asked.

"Why not? I enjoy good pizza as much as the next person."

Surprisingly, Owen spoke first. "Are you a person?" Then he glanced at the Recording Monitor and said, "Hey, why is that surprising?"

I stomped over to the Monitor and shifted the angle so he could no longer see it. Then I went into my spotless kitchen, placed several slices of pizza in the oven for reheating, and fetched the kids three cans of soda. I put the kettle on for myself.

"Yes, Owen, I am a person. I'm a member of the Historical Society. As with the other groups in the Knowledge Union, no Outsiders know of us. Most Union members don't know much about us either; it makes our work go more smoothly." I poured the soda into glasses and placed them on coasters in front of my guests.

"What is your work?" Simon asked.

"The Society records history as it happens, with different members observing different subjects. I specialize in chronicling the Order of Physics, which is why I'm stationed in Lawnville. The Chronicle I've been working on for the last week and a day is about you and your friends, Simon. I am observing and recording your story. These"—I gestured to the Viewing Screen and Recording Monitor—"are my tools. It appears that I am narrating the story of how you change the universe."

Simon sprayed a mouthful of soda all over my carpet.

"Don't worry; I'll clean that up later," I said, trying to hide my dismay. "I think I preferred it without company," I added in a low voice.

CHAPTER 31

GREYGOR GERYSON HAS HIS DAY

"Me?" Simon asked as he wiped the soda off his face. "Change the universe? How? Why me?"

I rubbed my chin. "I'm not certain. Even Narrators are only told what is needed to make a good Chronicle. I'll tell you this—no Outsider has ever seen Dunkerhook Woods before. Yet the Breeze invited you right in. Notice how Alysha and Owen could never find the woods without you? Alysha felt enough of the Breeze to lure her in that first time, but both only got the full Breeze treatment when you were all fleeing Veenie and Sirabetta. Now they should have no problem noticing the woods on their own. But Simon, the woods like you. The Book, too. Letting you access its wondrous formulas, humming when you hold it! Just having two Keepers at once is history being made. And I get to Chronicle it."

"So you follow Simon around all the time?" Owen asked.

"Not just Simon. I see what is needed for the Chronicle to be told right. As for following, only in a manner of speaking. I don't go anywhere, as I've said; the Viewing Screen can observe you wherever you go. Even off planet, if need be."

They sat silently (a rarity with these three); I could tell they were impressed.

"So wait, do you watch as we go to the bathroom?" Alysha asked.

Okay, maybe *she* wasn't as impressed as the other two. "No, dear. Have you ever read a book in which the characters go to the bathroom? Quite frankly, who wants to read about it?" My oven timer dinged. "Ah. Victuals!" I brought out four plates of pizza. "Enjoy! It'll help you get your strength back and should be just as tasty as if eaten in the restaurant. Or outside this apartment." I sighed.

As we ate, Alysha guessed that sitting in my apartment for so long had warped my brain. I couldn't help but lose my famous English reserve at that. "I am not bloody warped! I am merely expressing my pride in my work. And so what if I'm getting a bit dodgy from sitting here alone for so long? I'd like to see you try it!"

Too late, I realized what I'd done. "Oh, dear."

Alysha gasped. "You read my mind!"

I groaned. With all these rules being broken, I was bound to get stuck narrating infomercials as punishment. But as I liked to finish what I'd started, I continued. "Not quite: I can sense your surface thoughts, yes, but only those relevant to the Chronicle. After all, that is what Narrators do, correct? Especially in this type of Chronicle: a first person/third person omniscient tale. Only the best from Greygor Geryson."

All three kids asked, "Who?"

I blushed. "Er, that's me. That's my name."

"Wait," Simon said. "So you read Mermon Veenie's and Sirabetta's minds, too?"

I shook my head. "I'm afraid it doesn't work like that; I don't know why. I expect my Keeper knows the answer, but I've never met him. It's that whole never–leaving–here thing, I suppose. But when chronicling, I only know what I know and nothing more. I knew when Mermon was scared or anxious, but I could learn none of his plans about Sirabetta. And I know nothing of Sirabetta; I couldn't even get an emotional reading off her."

The kids frowned; they'd hoped for better information.

"I'd think you'd know all about someone like that with all her talk of revenge against the Orders," Owen said. "Or having such a loud voice in that hood."

I was beginning to feel quite cross, as if I wasn't being respected. I am a Narrator, not a detective! "Yes, well, it's not as simple as all that. Wait, what? Revenge against the Orders? She *did* say that, didn't she? And that hood. I believe her hooded black coat let her become invisible, rather than any tattoo formulas. That reminds me of something."

I gasped and rushed to my bookshelf, a well-organized collection of past Chronicles and Knowledge Union reference books (as well as some choice novels for when things get dull). I scanned the spines of the many volumes there and found a compendium of items created by the Orders.

"Here it is: the Overcoat of Dr. Solomonder Smithodrome!"

The three kids rushed over to me, crowding in to look at the book I held. I continued to read. "'Solomon Smith, doctor of Psychology . . . also known as Solomonder Smithodrome, Keeper of the Order of Psychology and honorary member of the Council of Sciences.'" I tapped the entry. "Yes, here we go. 'He designed his hooded Overcoat with the aid of the Craftsmen's Guild, incorporating an important psychological principle into its weave. It allows the wearer to go unseen when nobody knows he is there. Visibility is restored when the wearer's presence is reasonably suspected, and only to those who think he's there.' An odd bit of clothing. But it does explain why Sirabetta appeared whenever I saw Veenie talking to her or thought she was present."

"So how did Sirabetta get it from this Solomon?" Simon asked.

I coughed uncomfortably. "I'm really not supposed to get involved, and telling you that would be a bit too much information," I said, closing the book.

"But our lives are in danger," Simon said.

I frowned. "True, but I might lose my job."

Alysha put her hands on her hips. "You can't possibly care more about your job than our lives, could you? We're just kids!"

"Pushy kids. But no, I don't want to see you killed or hurt."

"Maybe this is fine," Owen said. "You think this has never happened, but you don't know *everything*. This might be part of your job. Maybe you'll be fired if you *don't* do it."

I rubbed my chin as I pondered that. "I'll see what I can find." I removed my spectacles as I searched my bookshelf for the correct reference book.

"Don't you need your eyeglasses?" Owen asked.

"The wretched things aren't real; I removed the lenses long ago."

"Then why wear them?" Alysha asked.

I blushed and looked away. "I wanted to look more like a proper Narrator."

I found a tome on recent events in the Council of Sciences and starting flipping through. I stabbed my finger at an index entry, turned to the page, and stopped in shock. "My, my. Here's an interesting fact: 'Dr. Smithodrome's wife, Sara Beth Smith, joined the Order a week after her husband did; she became Sirabetta Smithodrome.' As you've no doubt gathered, official membership in the Union involves a slight name change."

Simon's face paled. "So Sirabetta's in the Union?"

"Not anymore. Listen: 'In February 2005, Solomonder and Sirabetta were divorced and began feuding in the following months. By June 2005, Sirabetta had begun recruiting members of the Order of Psychology to help her overthrow Solomonder and let her take over as Keeper of the Order. She was defeated; her followers and she were—" He gasped and became even paler than normal. "They were stripped of their formulas and lost their Union Cards."

"Union Cards, what does that mean?" Owen said.

I felt my throat closing as I answered; this was not something I liked to think about, much less talk about. But they deserved to know. "Losing your Union Card is what we call being ejected from the Union. It's supposed to be *quite* rare, only for terrible crimes. The BOA has your memory partially erased and your life rearranged; you no longer remember the Union or have anything more to do with it." I paused. "In some extreme criminal cases, they send you to Outsider prison. That's what they did with Sirabetta, as Sara Beth Daly. That's her maiden name."

Owen gasped. "They threw her in jail—that's why she wants revenge!"

"Yeah, but you said she had no memory. Or formulas," Simon said.

Alysha frowned. "And where's this Solomonder guy now? Why'd he let her have his inviso–coat?"

I closed the reference book. "It doesn't say here. There are no further entries on either of them."

"You've got to call someone!" Simon said. "Tell people who Sirabetta is, find out what happened to Solomonder, and get the Order of Physics off our backs."

"Simon, I'm sorry; I cannot do anything more. I'm a Narrator, not a helper. I shouldn't have done this much. My purpose is just to sit and watch. If I don't know something, such as who that Miss Fanstrom woman really is, it's clearly not ready to be revealed in the Chronicle yet."

Alysha balled her hands into fists and opened her mouth, ready to make a threat, but Owen put a hand on her shoulder. I stared, stunned, as he said, "It's not his fault." He paused thoughtfully. "It's like fish asking a human to come underwater and help them. He can do it for as long as he holds his breath, but after that, he's got to go back up on land."

I took a step back, amazed. Who knew Owen could be so wise?

"Yeah?" Alysha said. "But then he can just get a snorkel or some scuba gear and go back down for longer!"

And then there was Alysha.

Simon shook his head. "I think Owen's right, Alysha. We've come this far on our own. We'll manage."

I nodded. "I can't see the future, but I can tell you this— you've accomplished more incredible things in a few days than most on Earth will ever do. And you've shown more bravery and cleverness than many Union members as well."

I frowned as Owen scarfed down the last slice of pizza,

which had been sitting on my plate. It looked like I'd be calling for more delivery soon.

"I can tell you one thing that may be helpful," I said. "Mountain Hospital, where Ralfagon is being kept and Eldonna is keeping watch? There's a shortcut that will keep you off the roads, away from Physics members if you're lucky."

"Where?" Simon asked.

"Through the woods, over that ravine," I said. "The path continues on to another entrance. Go out that way and down Mountain Road; you should reach Mountain Hospital easily. It's so rare that an Order member would need to go to the hospital that I doubt they know the shortcut. It might be your best hope."

Simon stood, and the others followed suit.

"Thanks, Mr. Narrator," Owen said. "I don't even feel tired anymore."

Alysha nodded. "Yeah, thanks, I guess. But if we get killed from this, I'm going to be really mad at you."

"Um, Greygor, right?" Simon asked. "If we do get out of this, maybe we'll come by again when I'm not the subject and you can talk more."

I shrugged. "We can work it out. I almost always have pizza around."

They left, and I started to clean Simon's soda mess from the carpet. I hoped that the information I'd given them would keep them alive; I also hoped that it would not get me in trouble.

CHAPTER 32

HAIL AND FAREWELL

I watched from my recliner as the kids left. Simon paused outside my apartment, wondering which was the best way out. Then he led his friends back the way they had come before. As they walked past a certain point, they found themselves back at school.

"Hey, it's Miss Fanstrom's office," Owen said. "How did that happen?"

Simon looked at the closed office door. "Maybe she left the teleportation device on." He knocked on her door, but there was no answer. "Guess she went home."

"Let's get to the hospital," Alysha said. They made their way through the school halls; by now, most teachers and students had gone home. The kids were so preoccupied with our meeting and their mission that they failed to consider a certain gym teacher.

I watched in horror as inside the gym, Willoughby Wanderby's cell phone rang and woke him. "Ohhh, my head," he mumbled before answering. "Yes?"

"Are you coming with us to the hospital?" a female voice asked. "It's visiting hours." Wanderby let out another groan. "What's wrong?" the woman asked.

Wanderby hesitated. "A small problem at the school. Nothing I can't handle."

Then Simon, Alysha, and Owen walked past the entrance to the gym, and Wanderby spotted them.

"You!" he snarled, dropping his cell phone. "This time you won't get away!" He ran into the hall.

Simon quickly spoke his friction formula, and Wanderby's feet slid out from under him. He landed hard on his butt and groaned.

"Owen, hit him with velocity. Quick!" Simon shouted.

Owen, already dizzy, went pale. "But he's a teacher!"

"It's him or us!" Alysha said. "Just knock him out."

Wanderby started to speak his rotational formula, but before he could finish, Owen used his velocity formula to hurl him down the hall. Wanderby slammed into a set of lockers and sank to the floor, unmoving.

"I don't think I'm getting a good grade in gym class this year," Owen said.

Unbeknownst to the kids (but painfully knownst to me), Wanderby's cell phone was lying open in the gym. "Willoughby? Willoughby?" the female voice shouted. "That's it; something's up. Set the Gateway for Wanderby's school!"

Simon, Owen, and Alysha ran out the nearest exit to the playground but stopped as a heavy downpour started suddenly. A handful of kids playing on the jungle gym squealed at the sudden heavy rain and ran off, drenched.

Owen groaned. "Great, it's been sunny all day and now this. I don't even have a jacket or an umbrella . . ."

Simon and Alysha grabbed Owen's arms and yanked him forward, toward the nearest break in the chain-link fence surrounding the playground.

Alysha noticed a bluish tinge to the puddles forming on the ground. She stopped. "What's with the rain?"

They all turned to look and gasped at the source of the rain's bluish hue. A beautiful, glowing rectangle had risen up in front of the school's outside brick wall. Before the kids could react, a leg stepped out of the blueness. It belonged to the lovely red-haired Loisana Belane of the Order of Physics. She emerged from the Gateway, followed by Myarina Myashah and Robertitus Charlsus.

Myarina frowned. "Stupid automatic rainstorm. This is ruining my hair."

"There was no time for raincoats," Loisana said.

Robertitus pointed at Simon and his friends as rain plastered his plaid shirtsleeve to his thick arm. "We've got worse problems than rain: Outsiders! We've been spotted!"

It was true. Although the rain was picking up in intensity, it was not yet hard enough to hide the Gateway and the Order members from sight.

Simon squinted. "Wait a second; I know that redheaded woman. She does the weather on the news. She came to the school last year to talk about meteorology!"

Owen gestured at Robertitus. "And that guy's a bowling instructor at Lawn Lanes on Route Four!"

Alysha studied Myarina. "The shorter woman runs a fashion workshop." Simon and Owen snickered. "What? Rachelle made me go." She paused. "Wait, what are they doing here?"

Loisana, Myarina, and Robertitus stood still, horrified at this breach in protocol. Loisana moaned. "This is my fault! I figured Wanderby was under attack, and I didn't wait until the rain got heavy enough."

The double doors of the school banged open and Wanderby stomped out with one hand clamped to his head. He noticed the Order members and, after a split-second hesitation, pointed at the kids. "Stop them!" he roared.

The kids started to run for the nearest exit, but Loisana spoke her formula and gestured toward them. The water froze; solid sheets of it coated the fence and blocked the three exits. The thin layer of water on the ground solidified, trapping the kids' feet. The falling rain became hail that pelted them.

Myarina cleared her throat. "Loisana, darling, while you're at it . . ." She gestured to the rain that was still soaking her friends and her.

Loisana spoke a variation on her formula, and the rain around the Order members dissolved into water vapor.

The kids tugged at their feet, trying to break free of the ice, and cried out from the painful hailstones. Loisana frowned and changed the hail back to rain; now the kids were just getting drenched.

"What happened?" Owen squealed.

"She's controlling states of matter," Simon said, "turning liquid into solid or gas. Freezing, vaporizing, melting."

"She can turn the rain into boiling-hot steam if she wants!" Alysha said.

Owen groaned. "This-is-bad-very-bad-terrible-bad!"

"Don't panic," Simon said. "The ice isn't too thick. Just keep tugging at your legs. I'm going to increase the gravity on the ice; it might become more brittle."

They could barely hear the adults talking over the downpour.

Loisana turned to Wanderby. "Okay, they're stopped. Now explain why you had me freeze three Outsider children."

"And why now?" Robertitus said in his thick southern drawl. "Loisana, Myarina, and me were just going to visit Ralfagon and Eldonna."

Wanderby winced at the lump on his head. "It's 'Myarina and I,'" he said.

Robertitus frowned. "You sure?"

"I *am* a teacher."

Loisana snorted. "You're a gym teacher, not a grammarian."

"Who cares?" Myarina snapped. "Let's get to the point here. This humidity is making my hair frizzy."

Wanderby hesitated. "I just need to talk to those three; you go on ahead."

Loisana narrowed her eyes. "I don't think so. What is this all about?"

"We haven't done anything wrong!" Simon yelled. "This is all a mistake!"

Wanderby shook his head. "Don't listen to them. They attacked Ralfagon."

"Three kids hospitalized the Keeper of Physics?" Loisana asked. "Please."

"They have formulas." Wanderby paused. "And the *Teacher's Edition*."

As if on cue, the Gateway closed and the rain stopped, leaving a layer of water on the ice spanning the playground.

Robertitus clenched his fists. "Then what are we waiting for? Let's get 'em!"

Alysha, still straining against the ice, said, "Okay, Owen, now you can panic."

CHAPTER 33

RUMBLE IN THE JUNGLE GYM

"Wait," Simon yelled out, "we didn't hurt anybody!"

"Except for Mr. Wanderby, but he started it," Owen said.

Alysha nodded. "Totally self-defense."

"Do you or do you not have the *Teacher's Edition*?" Wanderby hollered.

"Well, when you put it like that . . ." Owen said.

Wanderby gave an I-told-you-so look to his fellow Order members.

Loisana frowned at Wanderby (like me, she disliked I-told-you-so people), then turned to the kids. "Okay, give it here."

Simon managed to tug one foot free of the ice and

stomped at the other one. "It's not safe!" he shouted. "Not until we can get to the hospital."

"Why, so you can finish off Ralfagon?" Robertitus roared. "Not on my watch!" He spoke a formula and pointed at them, creating seismic waves that made the iced-over ground rumble and quake.

The seesaws pivoted, the huge concrete tubes quivered, and the tall metal jungle gym shimmied. The ice cracked around the kids' feet, and they fell to the heaving ground.

"You know, I had them trapped in that ice," Loisana said dryly.

Simon, Alysha, and Owen struggled to their feet and started for the nearest exit again. "Enough!" Wanderby bellowed. He pointed at the jungle gym. "Robertitus, cage them."

Robertitus redirected his formula, and more seismic waves rocked the metal structure. The ground beneath it bucked and kicked until the jungle gym snapped free and tipped over, imprisoning Simon, Alysha, and Owen between its bars.

"They're not listening," Alysha whispered. "We have to fight back."

"Okay, this thing is going zero g," Simon said. "Owen? Like yesterday."

Owen's voice took on a sudden fierceness. "Ready."

Simon canceled gravity on the jungle gym, and with great effort, the three heaved the massive metal structure over their heads.

Wanderby's mouth dropped open. "Now what do they think they're doing?"

"Rocket time!" Owen shouted. He spoke his formula and sent the jungle gym streaking through the air toward the school.

Simon returned the jungle gym's gravity so it had its full weight again, and the Order members barely managed to duck before the metal framework slammed into the school's brick wall. It cracked the wall and broke apart.

"Hey, that's school property!" Wanderby shouted.

But Owen wasn't listening; he used his velocity formula on the fractured pieces of jungle gym. The Order members ducked and dove, frantically trying to avoid the flying metal.

Wanderby used his rotational formula on Owen, viciously spinning him away, but Simon countered by increasing Owen's friction. The two formulas competed for control, making Owen wobble, but he was able to focus enough to clonk Wanderby on the head with a piece of jungle gym. It broke Wanderby's concentration, and his formula cut off abruptly.

Loisana glared at the kids and opened her mouth to attack, but Simon spoke his formula first; her frictionless feet slid out from under her and she fell flat on her back. With a quick friction shift, he made her stick to the ground.

"This is getting annoying," Myarina muttered. She spoke

her own formula and Simon, Alysha, and Owen were suddenly surrounded by huge mirrored walls. She was using light reflection to bounce their images back at them.

The kids felt like they were trapped in a giant mirrored box; they could only see their own images surrounding them. But as with a two-way mirror, the Order members could still see the kids perfectly—except for Loisana, who was still stuck to the ground. "Someone get me up," Loisana said. "This is embarrassing. And muddy."

Wanderby, unsteady from Owen's attack, leaned over to face her. "We have to take them down first, before they get out of that box. Can you freeze them?"

Loisana frowned. "I'll try, but I have to take water vapor from the atmosphere and turn it into water first; it's tricky to go right to ice if I can't see my target. Plus, it gives me brain freeze." She spoke her formula, and the air above the entire playground turned into water.

"You're getting us wet, too," Myarina whined.

"Then you're lucky I didn't just freeze everything first," Loisana replied, "or you'd all be a lot chillier."

Robertitus looked at the water accumulating on the playground and smiled. "Just what I needed." He generated more seismic waves, and each ground shift sent tidal waves of water toward the kids.

Simon, Alysha, and Owen were struggling to see through the reflective field when a six-foot-high wave of water sprang out of one wall and slammed them to the quivering ground.

Owen yelled over the roaring water, "Lower our gravity so we can jump out!"

Simon shook his head. "With the ground pitching like this, we couldn't control where we'd go!"

A concrete tube broke free of the tortured ground and rolled through the mirror illusion. The kids dove out of the way, only to get smacked by another wave.

Alysha grabbed Simon and Owen. "Get in the tube!" she yelled. They hurried inside and Simon used friction to hold the tube down. Although the concrete still moved with the rocking ground, it couldn't roll away—it was stuck fast to its patch of wet, icy dirt.

Inside the shelter of the tube, Owen asked, "Did you see? The tube and the waves went through the mirror. The walls aren't solid; we can go through them!"

"You're right!" Alysha said. "I've got an idea: when I leave, get on top of this thing, and whatever you do, stay out of the water on the ground. Can either of you do something to distract them?"

"I can try to throw water in their direction," Owen said. "I'll send it over your head at them. Let's see how *they* like it!"

"I can increase the gravity by the school to slow them down," Simon said. "But it'll hit you, too, when you get close."

"That's okay," she said. "I'll be prepared. Ready?" Alysha reached her hand out to them, palm down.

Simon and Owen just stared. "Why are you showing us your nails?" Owen asked.

Alysha rolled her eyes. "Haven't you guys *ever* watched sports? Put your hands on top of mine, then we'll say . . . oh, never mind. Just kick some butt."

Owen put his hand on top of hers. "Major butt!"

Simon put his on top of Owen's. "Colonel butt!"

Alysha sighed. "You are *so* corny. It's always the quiet ones."

CHAPTER 34

A SHOCK TO THE SYSTEM

I leaned forward in my recliner and cheered as Alysha went into action. This was the best Chronicle ever!

Wanderby narrowed his eyes to see through the falling water. "That girl just came out of the tube. Loisana, get ready to freeze her."

Simon spoke his gravity formula before Loisana could act; Wanderby, Myarina, and Robertitus collapsed to the ground, and Loisana couldn't concentrate enough to attack. Simon had made their area's gravity three times as heavy, so their every movement was a pained struggle.

It was a strain for Simon to concentrate on an area he couldn't see. He still managed to increase Owen's friction, allowing him to climb atop the water-slicked tube. Owen also had to struggle to focus his velocity control on the falling water; liquids were much harder to control than solids. He managed to collect a steadily growing puddle in the air above Simon and him.

Alysha dove forward through the mirror. For a second, she saw nothing; she was in the middle of the light wall. Then she burst through and saw the whole playground again. She dropped to her hands and knees to cope with the heaving ground and waves of water. She grinned as the Order members struggled with their increased weight. They were too busy to pay much attention to her.

Robertitus, the biggest and strongest, strained to get to his feet and prepared to send his seismic waves against Alysha. He struggled to maintain focus on her but had barely managed to aim his attack when Owen sent a water blob the size of a small swimming pool hurtling over Alysha's head. It crashed into Robertitus and the other Order members at three times its normal force, strengthened by the increased gravity. Robertitus was slammed into the brick wall and slid down, stunned. Myarina and Wanderby were flattened to the ground while Loisana, still friction-stuck down, had the wind knocked out of her.

All four Order members were momentarily helpless, sprawled onto dirt that was covered with water and segments of metal from the shattered jungle gym.

And Alysha had learned that water containing dissolved

particles from dirt is an excellent conductor of electricity. As is metal.

Alysha, still on her hands and knees, felt the extra gravity hit her. It didn't matter: she'd gotten as close as she needed to. She'd already built up a strong charge; now she grabbed hold of the nearest piece of metal, partially immersed in the water, and spoke her formula.

The air was filled with a loud popping sound as Alysha's stored electricity streaked through the water and metal, zapping the four adults. Suddenly, the ground stopped shaking, the water stopped dropping from the air, and the mirrored walls disappeared. The playground was eerily quiet.

Simon and Owen shut down their formulas. Exhausted, they dropped off the concrete tube and unsteadily crossed the ruined playground toward Alysha. She was shaky as she pointed to the adults. "I didn't know I had that much juice stored up." Her voice quivered. "Do you think they'll be . . . okay?"

Owen went to Myarina and, mimicking paramedics from the medical shows he'd watched on television, felt for a pulse at her jawline. "She's alive. Her pulse is strong." He went from one to the next, checking the same way, and announced that all four Order members were fine, just unconscious.

Alysha laughed nervously, still a little scared by what she'd done. "Listen to you. 'Her pulse is strong.' You should get a job at the hospital."

Simon nodded to Alysha. "Nice work."

Alysha shrugged. "We had to stop them somehow, right?"

"We tried to make them listen, but they wouldn't," Owen said.

"We did what we had to," Simon said.

Alysha exhaled slowly. "I'm just glad you didn't make some lame joke."

Simon grinned. "Shocking, isn't it?"

Alysha shook her head. "That's it. You're next."

They all laughed, overcome with relief and weariness. "Let's get out of here before they wake up or someone else comes after us," Simon said.

Owen nodded. "Or we have to clean up."

Alysha walked over to Myarina and Loisana. "Give me a second." While Simon and Owen retrieved their backpacks, Alysha bent over, her back to Simon and Owen, and rooted through the women's purses. Then she fished around in the water for a few minutes. "Okay, I'm ready."

She took her backpack from Owen and poured something from her hands into the bag. Owen noticed. "What was that?" he asked.

"An insurance policy," Alysha said. "I'll explain later."

Simon reached into his bag. "Can you believe it? The Book isn't even wet!"

"We have to get to the hospital quickly," Owen said. "I do *not* want to face Mr. Wanderby in gym tomorrow."

They came to the fence. All the exits were still iced over:

Loisana's barriers had cracked but not shattered during the fight. Owen groaned. "No way can I climb that now."

"Owen, do you think you could manage a little more velocity control? 'Cause if you can, there's a great way to get to the woods," Simon said.

Simon negated their gravity, and Owen used velocity to lift and send them whooshing through the air. Simon let out a whoop of joy. Weary and scared or not, they were actually flying!

CHAPTER 35

LIKE FATHER, LIKE SON

Not long before that, Marcus Van Ny stirred at the sound of his cell phone ringing; he realized he'd dozed off in the nurse's office. The last thing he remembered was getting a few bandages and being told to lie down while the nurse called his father to come get him.

"Dad?" Marcus said as he answered his phone groggily. "You here yet?"

"I'm outside in the car," Myron Van Ny growled. "Hurry up."

Marcus sat up. The nurse wasn't there. "I just have to get my books from my locker."

"I do *not* have time for this," Myron practically roared.

"You have *no* idea how many important things I have to do right now."

Before Marcus could answer, he felt a rumbling and heard a distant crashing sound. "Did you feel that? Or hear it?"

"A man doesn't buy a car as luxurious as mine when he wants to see or hear anything outside," Myron snarled. "So no." With that, Myron hung up.

Marcus went to his locker; it was down the hall from Alysha's and Simon's . . . the same hall that led to the playground. He was surprised to see the school nurse—a kind, elderly man that Marcus couldn't stand. He was staring at the double doors to the playground, trying to see through a mysteriously cracked window.

"Hey! What's the big idea leaving me there by myself?" Marcus shouted. "I could have slipped into a coma or something!"

The nurse turned around, his face pale with fright. "Something's going on."

There was another rumble, this one fiercer and longer than the last; it was followed by another and another. "Is it an earthquake?" Marcus gasped.

"I don't know; there's tons of water outside! I don't want to get near it."

Marcus snorted. "That's because you're a wuss," he muttered under his breath. He walked over to the double doors, but a loud popping noise made him pause; he was sure he smelled something burning. He waited a few minutes to be sure the noise and shaking were done before putting his face to a window.

"Whoa. It's like a movie," Marcus said, marveling over the wreckage on the playground. And something more. "No way!" he exclaimed.

The nurse ran over to the other window. "What? What?"

Marcus pushed open the door and stared in horror and awe. He jumped as his cell phone rang, and he quickly answered. "Dad?"

"Boy, are you coming or not?"

"Dad, the playground's destroyed! Like a bomb went off, but there's water all over. And four people lying on the ground." He moved closer. "Is that Mr. Wanderby? My gym teacher!" He stared into the distance. "I swear I can see three kids flying! Oh no, it's them!" Marcus's knees went weak, and his voice rose in pitch. "They used witchcraft on me in gym today, too."

"Say that again?" Myron's voice was suddenly intense and focused. "Witchcraft? Flying? Who are these kids, Marcus? Where are they flying to?"

Marcus spoke in gasps, on the verge of hyperventilating. "Their names are Simon, Owen, and Alysha. And they're going toward the edge of Lawnville. The Stoneridge side."

"Dunkerhook Woods!" Myron's voice was a scratchy whisper.

"What woods? No, that loser Simon lives that way."

Myron laughed. "Of course! It's all clear now!"

"Dad? Can you come and get me?"

"Find another way home, boy," Myron growled. "This is it. This is it!"

Myron Van Ny, known to some as Mermon Veenie, disconnected the call and quickly dialed another number. "Sir? It's Veenie. I know where the kids are going with the Book!" Then he laughed cruelly as he sped off in the direction of the woods.

CHAPTER 36

ONCE MORE INTO THE WOODS, OLD FRIENDS

Owen paid close attention to his velocity control to steer them, making sure they stayed higher than people's houses but low enough to use the trees and roofs as cover. He didn't dare move them too fast; he was tired, and his reaction time was off. He was afraid he'd send them plowing into something.

Still, it was an exhilarating ride as the wind rushed past and the world slid away beneath them.

"Why don't we fly all the way to Mountain Hospital?" Alysha shouted.

"Can't!" Owen shouted back. "I'll pass out if I don't take us down soon." In fact, they were starting to wobble as they flew; they were barely aloft by the time Owen brought them to their destination: the end of Van Silas Way.

Simon increased their gravity as they settled to the street; curiously, the pavement was as wet as they were. None noticed the rain clouds dissipating during what was otherwise a sunny day.

The bruised, wet kids stood there and stared at the entrance to the woods. As I had predicted, all three could see it now.

"I'm not sure about this new wet look," a musical voice said.

Simon, Alysha, and Owen whipped around and found Flangelo, in human form, walking toward them from up the street. "Relax, commandos. The war's over for now. Nice fighting. You've all come a long way."

Alysha fumed. "You watched us go through all that and didn't try to help?"

Flangelo flung his hands up into the air. "For the last time, spark plug, I am not a fighter. I recognize how silly it sounds to say this to twelve-year-olds, but trust me, you are much tougher than I am. You even flew here faster."

"Don't worry about it," Simon said. "We did okay on our own. And I'm still eleven, by the way."

"You did great," Flangelo said in a tone more serious than he'd ever used with the kids before. "But it's not over. I followed to warn you. When your pals from the Order wake up, they're going to call for reinforcements. And after all that, I'm guessing you'll be too tired to use your formulas much more."

"Actually, I learned one more formula that I haven't used," Simon said.

"Oh, thank you!" Alysha said with relief. "I thought we were going to be relying on mine."

"So what's your formula?" Owen asked. "What can you do?"

"That's the problem; it's hard to understand. I'm pretty sure I won't be able to control it."

Owen and Alysha slumped. Flangelo cleared his throat. "I'm not in a position to throw stones here—I mean, I'm basically a chicken in sparrow's clothing—but wouldn't it have been better to, oh, I don't know, pick a formula you *did* understand?"

"I asked the Book what to pick and this is what it chose. It's called space–time and has to do with theoretical physics. Relativity."

"You mean like aunts and uncles?" Owen asked.

Flangelo groaned. "Oh, Scooter, just when you were starting to impress me."

"Albert Einstein had this whole theory-of-relativity thing," Alysha said. "Ever hear of $E = mc^2$?"

Owen shrugged. "Maybe."

"Alysha, do you know what it means?" Simon asked.

She shook her head.

"I talked to my dad about it; a little, I mean."

"Your dad?" Flangelo chirped.

"Rocket scientist," Alysha said.

"Sure," Flangelo said. "It's not brain surgery, but it'll do."

Simon thought about what his dad had said. Maybe he could teleport himself and his friends, but how could he control it? They could wind up halfway in the ground, or on the surface of the sun, or in the year 3012.

"No," Simon said, "it's still too risky. We should just go on foot."

Flangelo whistled sadly. "Good luck with that. With everything." He nodded solemnly and then turned into a bird and flew off.

Alysha watched him flap away. "My hero."

"C'mon, guys. We can't waste any more time," Simon said.

They stepped into Dunkerhook Woods, and the Breeze washed over them. Its energies flooded them more than ever before, imparting as much power as it could to their weakened bodies. They were almost able to forget how tired they were.

Owen breathed deeply and held up his hand. He concentrated, spoke his formula, and made a stone leap into his palm. "I think we just got recharged!"

"Thank you, Breeze!" Alysha whispered. "But don't use it up, Owen. What if we run into someone between here and the hospital?"

"Even that Eldonna might try to fight us when we show up," Simon said.

"So, let's-come-up-with-something-make-a-plan, you know, just in case," Owen said.

After several minutes of walking and strategizing, they reached the clearing and paused. "We're not far from the gap," Simon said. "We'll have to get across it without wasting too much formula strength. This is where it gets dangerous again."

"Danger? Big deal," Owen said. "I kicked Marcus's and Barry's butts in dodgeball, knocked my gym teacher around, and ate great pizza. I've led a full life."

Simon chuckled. "Okay, this is it. We stick together and follow the plan." Alysha and Owen nodded, and they headed on toward the ravine.

But they'd only gone a few feet when a familiar, chilling voice boomed. **"It's about time. I was starting to doze off."**

CHAPTER 37

HER FINAL OFFER

Simon, Alysha, and Owen froze as Sirabetta became visible; she was leaning on a tree down the path between them and the chasm. She was wearing her hood and sucking on a soda through a straw. (At least it looked like she was sucking on the straw; the thin plastic tube disappeared into the cavernous darkness of her hood.)

"Seriously, kids, could you move any slower?" She gestured past them. **"Veenie and I got here by Gateway at least ten minutes ago."**

I gulped; that explained all the puddles on Van Silas Way!

The kids looked to where Sirabetta pointed and saw

Mermon Veenie step onto the trail from behind a tree. He was between them and the Van Silas entrance to the woods, blocking off any chance of them going back the way they came. They were trapped.

Sirabetta sighed, the hood distorting the sound so it resembled a humming refrigerator. She tossed back her hood. "Ah, now I can see you better."

Mermon's teeny-tiny eyes narrowed microscopically, and he growled at the kids, "I don't care that you three turned my son Marcus into a whimpering mess and the laughing-stock of your gym class. I don't even care that you made me look like a fool on Saturday. If you give me the Book, you may live to see puberty."

Sirabetta arched a beauteous eyebrow. "Give *you* the Book, Veenie?" she called out. "Don't tell me you're going to pull one of those last-minute power-struggle things; it's so trite."

Mermon's eyes widened to the size of nickels, which, for them, was huge. "Of course not, Sir. You know I'm loyal."

"Yes, like a faithful dog with rabies," she said. "Don't fret; once I've mastered the *Teacher's Edition* and gotten these tat-toos off my skin, you and your confederates will get the power you crave."

"You're pretty calm," Alysha said. "I figured you'd be in a much worse mood after Simon and Owen kicked your butts."

Sirabetta's smile vanished. "Aren't you sweet? No, wait, you're not." She pulled up a corner of her coat, revealing several purplish bruises among the tattoos. "Your friend's trick with gravity gave me this new color scheme. I'm not a fan. But want to know why I'm so cheerful?"

Simon, Alysha, and Owen nodded nervously.

Sirabetta pointed to a half-green, half-yellow tattoo on her other knee. "A painkiller formula! I first chose it to help me deal with the strain of all these tattoos, but it works just fine on injuries. Unfortunately, it doesn't work while I'm using another formula. Worsening pain makes me cranky, and when I'm cranky, things get blown up. So why don't you do the smart thing? I *know* you've had a rough day and your paltry few formulas are all but used up. And I *know* you will be screaming in agony in a few minutes if you don't hand over my Book."

"So what's your plan after that, Sara Beth?" Simon asked.

Mermon's jaw dropped. "That's your real name?"

"Shut up, Veenie." Sirabetta frowned. "You kids have been doing some research, hmm?"

Sirabetta looked up into the sky, as if she could actually see me watching from my apartment. I shuddered and snacked nervously on a scone.

Simon continued, "Is it because you're mad at your ex-husband? Is that what this is all about?"

Sirabetta crossed her arms. "Is this your way of staving off terror, boy?"

"Do you always answer a question with a question?" Owen asked.

"And even the tiny one shows a backbone," Sirabetta said. "Trying to find out the villain's plot before she kills you? So overdone. But I'll tell you this . . . once I have that Book, I'll get rid of all the Physics formulas I'm wearing and have all that power without the pain. I'll get the other Books, one by one, until I've toppled the Council of Sciences. Then I can turn my attention to the rest of the Knowledge Union. And I will have my revenge." She seemed to concentrate very hard on not cackling evilly and, with great effort, succeeded. She got away with only a villainous glint in her eyes.

"It's your own fault!" Alysha shouted. "You tried to take over the Order of Psychology!"

Sirabetta waved a fist. "Solomonder had it coming! After we divorced, he started excluding me from the Order. He made me feel like I didn't belong. I couldn't stand for that. Did you know that there is no protocol for a transfer? I had no way of leaving the Order of Psychology for another Order or group even if I wanted to. Even if I was willing to give up on psychology, which was my life. I grew up loving the science of the mind, but I would've left and found another Order if it meant I could stay in the Union. No chance, though; I was stuck."

She paused and looked away. "What choice did I have?" Her angry tone had turned sad. "I didn't *want* to be a villain, but it was the only way out of my misery. And when my rebellion was put down, I was kicked to the side. Left to rot."

"But you were supposed to forget about the Order and

go to prison and all that!" Owen said. "So how are you here?"

Sirabetta folded her arms proudly. "I am no fool, child. I didn't stage my revolt without a good backup plan. And if you're in the Order of Psychology, you learn the best mental tricks. They do wonders for resisting mind wipes or sneaking past guards in Outsider prisons."

"Fine, they were jerks, but that's no excuse to act like a maniac!" Alysha yelled.

Sirabetta shook her head. "Maniac? It's not like I've killed anybody . . . yet." She grinned cruelly. "You know why the Board of Administration didn't lift a finger when Solomonder did what he did? The only way they'll directly intervene with an Order is if the Keeper dies. And that's why I won't kill Solomonder until I'm absolutely ready. I can't kill Ralfagon and you, Simon; the entire BOA would know. Though after all your open formula use, they're bound to investigate sooner or later. The Union is very focused on secrecy."

"For now," Mermon sneered.

"That's right, Veenie. Once I'm ready, when I have all the power I need, I'll be able to ignore all the Union's precious rules. I'll change the entire system so that what happened to me can't happen again. If the Union doesn't accept me, I'll be viewed as a tyrant. I can live with that. But *I* will be fair. *I* will be just."

"What about the tattoos?" Simon asked. "How'd you do that?"

Sirabetta shook her head. "No. I'm keeping some secrets. Now, my patience is gone, and this painkiller formula is keeping me only so pleasant." She sighed. "I don't want to have to fight you; I don't want to hurt you. I won't even try to strip you of your powers and control your life, like the Order of Physics would do if they got hold of you. But I've suffered and sacrificed too much to let you stop me now. So I'll make you one final offer, young Simon. Emphasis on *final*. Give me the Book, or your friends will get a free ride on a lightning bolt. Your choice."

Alysha folded her arms and glared at Sirabetta. "We've had enough of your whole 'bad guy with a purpose' routine. A crybaby story, if you ask me."

Owen reached down to the ground and picked up a thick branch. "You want the Book, you come and get it, lady."

Simon smiled. "You heard them. I'm sorry about what you went through, but a bully's a bully. The Book stays with me."

Sirabetta rubbed at her glowing painkiller tattoo and frowned. "So be it." She gestured toward Simon. "Veenie, just stun or wound him, but I want to see the others in ashes."

CHAPTER 38

It's All Fun and Games Until Someone Gets Hit by Lightning

Mermon showed his teeth with a smile that would put most sharks to shame. He spoke his formula and pointed at the kids. As a bluish glow formed around his hands, Alysha spoke her own formula.

A sonic boom split the air as a bolt of lightning blasted out from Mermon Veenie's fingertips. A jagged blue-and-white streak as thick as his arm seared the air as it leapt toward the kids. Alysha's formula drew it off course, and it veered to her as if she were a human lightning rod.

The bolt struck her chest with a terrible crackling sound. Alysha cried out in surprise, but she wasn't hurt. Every bit of the lightning's electrical charge soaked into her, leaving her unharmed.

Mermon was baffled; this was not how lightning was supposed to behave. He changed the wording of his formula, and his entire body was surrounded by that bluish glow. With the altered command, he gathered an immense electrical charge in his body. This time, the lightning burst out of every inch of him, from hair to heels. It was more than an entire thundercloud could generate, and he unleashed it all at once. This was a mistake.

A six-foot-four-inch-high, two-foot-wide onslaught of sizzling electrical power tore through the air with a deafening roar. Alysha, Owen, and a chunk of the forest should have been vaporized, but again, the attack was sucked into Alysha. She gritted her teeth and clenched her fists as her entire body was enveloped by Veenie's blindingly intense energy. With her formula activated, she kept draining everything Veenie had.

By the time Veenie realized what was happening, it was too late. He couldn't reverse his formula—the floodgates were jammed open. He cried out until his voice cracked as he was drained of all electrical power.

At last the lightning flow stopped, leaving Veenie's once-immaculate suit charred and blackened. Wisps of smoke curled out from his body. His tiny eyes were unfocused, his mouth drooped, and he stood unsteadily.

Sirabetta stared in confusion. "Veenie? What happened?"

Simon glanced at Alysha, her entire body glowing bluish white with energy, and she gave him a thumbs-up.

"Owen, now!" Simon shouted.

Owen didn't bother with his formula. Instead, he raised his branch, yelled fiercely, and charged at Veenie.

Veenie, dazed, had no chance to react before the thick branch smacked into his stomach. He pitched forward, and Owen brought the branch down on his back, hard. The branch snapped in two from the impact, but Owen didn't stop. He took both halves, one in each hand, and pounded away like a drummer doing a solo.

"Stop it, you brat!" Sirabetta hissed. She pulled one sleeve back and scanned the tattoos, preparing to unleash some terrible attack on him.

Simon nodded to Alysha. Alysha plunged her hands into her bag and pulled out assorted coins, screws, and other small pieces of metal she'd taken from Myarina's and Loisana's purses and the playground battlefield. Filled to the bursting point with electricity, she spoke the command words to release her electrical charge. She poured much of her stored-up energy into the metal and threw both handfuls at Sirabetta.

Sirabetta stopped her tattoo search and instinctively raised her arms as the glowing projectiles struck her, the path, and the forest around her. She screamed as each tiny object released massive bursts of blinding blue-white energy on impact, blowing huge holes into the trail and tearing apart surrounding trees.

The explosions were over in a few seconds, leaving an astonished Simon, Alysha, and Owen staring in awe at the cloud of smoke and dust.

"I didn't think it would be so much," Alysha whispered hoarsely. "What did I *do* to her?"

The woods' trademark Breeze kicked in, clearing away the haze and revealing a twelve-foot-wide, four-foot-deep crater that now lay across the path.

To the kids' horror, Sirabetta was standing, unhurt, in the middle of it.

CHAPTER 39

The Last Stand

Sirabetta coughed and looked down at what was left of her hooded coat. "You idiots!" she spat. "Do you have any idea how hard it was to steal that thing?" She smacked at the smoldering fabric, and it collapsed into a pile of ash at her feet. "Now it's only fit for a dustpan."

Underneath, Sirabetta was wearing a formfitting, black rubber outfit like a wet suit. It left her arms exposed to the shoulder and her legs bare to midthigh, revealing her scores of tattoos and more bruises from their earlier fight.

Sirabetta took a deep, calming breath as the painkilling formula on her other knee began to glow again. "A good try, though. Too bad for you I've got this." She pointed to another half-green, half-yellow tattoo just above her left elbow. "It activates on contact, insulating my body against electricity." She shrugged. "When you ally yourself with a dog like Mermon Veenie, you take precautions."

Simon recovered from his surprise quickly and reached into his backpack, whipping out his paintball gun.

Sirabetta snorted. "Child, this is not the time for toys." Then she yelped with pain as Simon started firing—like I said, those paintballs really sting when they hit bare skin. He managed to get off several shots before Sirabetta spat out a formula and snapped her fingers. The resulting air pressure explosion destroyed the gun and sent Simon sprawling onto the ground.

"You little brat!" Sirabetta yelled. "What did that accomplish besides annoying me?" Then she looked down at her legs, where most of Simon's shots had struck. There were splotches of fresh paint covering numerous tattoos. "No! What have you done?"

She swiped at the paint and managed to smear some off, but the damage was done. Enough of her tattoos were covered, including the silver explosive one and the one she'd used to generate heat. Until she could get that paint off, she couldn't read them—those formulas were useless.

"That's it? Did you really think that would stop me?" Sirabetta said.

Instead of answering her, Simon looked to Alysha and Owen. "Go!" he yelled.

Alysha pulled the remaining metal items from her pockets and poured what was left of Veenie's electrical energy into them. They couldn't hurt Sirabetta, but there were other ways to use them.

Simon concentrated and shifted his gravity control, using a variation on an old trick.

Owen saw only one useful weapon around him and grabbed at it with his velocity formula.

Suddenly, Sirabetta was besieged from all sides. Simon had altered gravity just as he had during the battle in the street, making Sirabetta the center of attraction for the loose items in the woods. She swatted and kicked at sticks and stones that streaked toward her.

As Sirabetta dodged a zooming rock, she also had to dive away from Alysha's strikes. Electrical bombs struck thick branches or small trees' trunks, making them falling hazards. Everywhere Sirabetta turned, heavy chunks of wood dropped toward her. Even when she dodged these tree parts, Simon's formula added them to the growing collection of objects that fell toward her.

Owen's assault was the hardest to avoid, though. He used velocity to hurl the unconscious Veenie at Sirabetta. Mermon Veenie was tall and heavy, and every time he zoomed past, Sirabetta had to duck or leap out of the way.

Sirabetta snarled; she was getting tired and battered. After swatting a cluster of speeding leaves away from her face, she read a yellow tattoo on her shoulder: her deforestation formula. The leaves crumbled to ash just before they could hit her again.

"Enough!" she yelled. A large piece of tree trunk fell toward her head, but she quickly redirected her formula. The trunk smoldered and crumbled into several small fragments that fell around her. The fragments were still at the mercy of the changed gravity, though, so they smacked into her from all sides.

Owen sent Veenie zooming toward her again, and this time, Veenie started to wake up. "Sir, what is happening?" he cried.

Sirabetta leapt out of the way again, but Veenie's shoe smacked her shoulder painfully as he zipped past. Sirabetta screamed in pain and grabbed Veenie's body, using it as a shield.

"Sir, what are you do—" was all Veenie had time to whine before a chunk of shattered tree thudded on his head. Once again, he was knocked out.

Sirabetta struggled to hold Mermon up, using his body to block incoming projectiles. With him shielding her, she had time to search her arms and legs for the tattoo she wanted.

Owen tried to send Veenie, with Sirabetta holding on tightly, flying toward one of the nearby trees. Nothing happened. A second later, Owen winced and sagged for-ward; he'd used his formula too much. He had no velocity control left.

Simon tried to increase the gravity pull toward Sirabetta so everything would fall toward her faster and hit her harder. He felt a pop inside his head and gasped. The tree fragments, stones, branches, and leaves clinging to Sirabetta fell to her feet. Sirabetta, realizing what happened, dropped Mermon to the dirt, too. Various bits of forest, now obeying normal gravity, dropped onto his unconscious body.

Simon tried gravity again, but nothing happened. He had overused it.

Sirabetta was winded from having to hold Veenie's body up for so long. Between heavy breaths, she shouted across the distance between them. "What's the matter, children? Pushed yourselves too hard?" She smiled cruelly as her pain-reliever tattoo flooded her with comfort. "So much for your heroic last stand. Ready to lie down yet?"

Simon, Owen, and Alysha looked at one another. "How bad?" Simon asked.

Owen shook his head. "I'm out."

Alysha cracked her knuckles. "Little bit left."

"Any thoughts?" Simon asked with a sigh.

Owen gritted his teeth. "No way do we let her win this."

Alysha nodded. "No way some blonde in a wet suit pushes us around."

Simon took a deep breath. "Here's the *real* last stand, then."

Alysha threw the last of her metal—two pennies—filled with her remaining electrical charge. They hit the ground in front of Sirabetta and the prone Veenie, exploding and kicking up a cloud of dirt that temporarily blinded Sirabetta.

Simon pointed to Alysha's and Owen's feet as a signal and poured all his concentration into one last use of friction. The three friends streaked forward, their feet gliding smoothly over the trail, and got ready to strike with the only weapons they had left. Owen gripped the two branch halves he'd used to clobber Veenie, Simon cocked his backpack (with a few textbooks and the Book inside), and Alysha balled up her fists. They came from three sides in the hope that one would get in a lucky shot.

Sirabetta coughed and waved at the dust around her enough to see the kids sliding toward her. She read her air pressure formula; the tattoo glowed bright blue as the air exploded, tossing her attackers away like they were toys.

Owen got hit hardest. He was flung up into the air and landed with an audible *thud* in the crater behind Sirabetta.

Alysha, moving in from the right, was thrown straight back into the woods. She tore through several bushes before crashing into a tree trunk. She collapsed to the ground and lay on the forest floor, unmoving.

Simon, coming in from the left side, was flung up into the trees. He plowed through several small branches and grabbed hold of a thick tree limb before he could fall back down.

"And then there was one." Sirabetta exhaled. "That was good. A noble effort." She grimaced and looked up at Simon.

"What next? Do I have to torture you? You've hurt me, you've blocked some of my tattoos, but I have plenty left. More than enough to keep you in agony for hours. But you know it hurts me every time. And I don't *want* to do any of this. Be reasonable, Simon. Let's take the easy road."

Simon didn't answer; it took all his fading strength to cling to that tree limb.

Sirabetta looked at her right shoulder, reading the yellow formula for deforestation. The tree limb withered and finally disintegrated. Simon fell eight feet to the dirt floor and cried out as he landed badly on his left arm.

Simon lay moaning while Sirabetta approached. She looked down at him and smirked. "And this is my prize." She reached for Simon's backpack.

A loud burst of birdsong filled the air. Sirabetta whirled around as a flock of sparrows zipped through the trees and surged toward her. "Oh, what now?" she snarled.

One bird's chirp, louder than the others', sounded mysteriously like "Charge!" The birds dive-bombed Sirabetta, wildly pecking, clawing, and flapping at her. (Had Owen been able to see, he would have been satisfied to know it very much resembled Alfred Hitchcock's *The Birds*.) Sirabetta was driven back from Simon, shrieking in pain every time a claw or beak hit.

After several moments of uselessly smacking at her avian assailants, Sirabetta ducked down and covered her head. Her muffled words were barely audible, but the result was clear.

A beach–ball–size sphere of multicolored light sprang into existence above her and tossed brilliantly hued rays in every direction.

The birds twittered in confusion, blinded by the raging rainbow. Most of them collided with one another, the trees, or the ground. Sirabetta repeated her air pressure formula, and the explosion threw the remaining sparrows in every direction.

One last bird dropped to the dirt, blurred, and transformed into Flangelo. He moaned in pain and then was silent.

Sirabetta shrieked with fury and pain as she examined the damage. Her rubber wet suit was torn in many places, and several more tattoos had been pecked beyond recognition. One of them was her painkiller tattoo. She staggered over to Simon. Her voice was ragged and hoarse. "For this pain, boy, you should suffer. But first . . ." Once more, she bent over to his backpack.

"Ahhh!" she suddenly squealed.

Simon wasn't ready to give up; though it hurt to even move, he had lurched forward and clamped his teeth onto her ankle.

Sirabetta stamped at Simon, kicking him with her other bare foot until he let go and lay stunned. "Don't you know it's over? Don't you know you've lost?" She looked along her arms, choosing from the remaining tattoos. "Then let me make it clear." She read a tattoo on her left wrist, and it glowed a sickly bright green.

Simon curled into a ball, holding his stomach with his one good arm. His belly quivered as if he'd eaten five chili dogs with onions and ridden the fastest looping roller coaster in the world. Twice. His internal heaving increased, and a vile taste rose up his throat. He squirmed as a nauseated feeling tore him from the inside out, leaving him paralyzed with that about-to-throw-up sensation.

"That's another from Biology," Sirabetta said. "Utter nausea. You can't concentrate enough to use a formula if you're trying not to vomit." She grimaced, fighting her own pain; the strain from her tattoos and injuries was clearly wearing her down.

For a moment, the woods were quiet but for the sound of Simon gagging. Sirabetta gritted her teeth. "I can handle this. I can finish what I started." She clenched and unclenched her fists, then exhaled. "I have earned this."

She pulled the *Teacher's Edition* out from Simon's backpack. "Hello, gorgeous. Meet your new master."

The Book shuddered in her grasp, as if trying to break free. "Fight it all you want, you rebellious tome," Sirabetta said. "You can't resist me." She revealed a multicolored spiral tattooed into her other palm. "*This* says you can't."

(I gasped—that was the mark of the Board of Administration! How could she have gotten a tattoo from them?)

Sirabetta nodded to Simon. "Don't worry, boy, this tattoo works independently from the others; it won't interrupt your anguish."

Sirabetta turned away from Simon and took a few steps as she touched her tattooed palm to the *Teacher's Edition's* clasp. The metal sprang open the instant her palm made contact, and the Book stopped struggling.

Sirabetta held it over her head. "It worked. They said it would, and it did. At the risk of sounding cliché"—she laughed with delirious glee—"at last! At last it is mine!"

Several feet from Sirabetta, Simon stopped trying to fight the nausea. Using his good arm, he stuck a finger down his throat and made himself throw up. He gasped for air and, for just a few seconds, was free from the formula.

Desperate, he did the only thing he could think of. He didn't know what would happen, but it was his last chance, and he took it. He spoke the words of his third formula— space–time—and aimed it at Sirabetta.

Sirabetta felt the effect at once. "What . . . what are you doing to me?" She screamed but was unable to move. She stood frozen, still holding the *Teacher's Edition* above her head. Her entire body began to ripple, as if made of water. "What is this? WHAT IS HAPPENING?"

As she screamed, her voice rose higher and higher and her body shuddered. There was a burst of bright white light and the air was filled with the dusty smell of space–time bending. There was no sound, though. Whatever was happening didn't involve any air ripping.

Within seconds, the light faded. Where there had been a beautiful woman of thirty or so years, there was now a pretty girl about Alysha's age. Simon had reversed the flow of time around Sirabetta!

Reeling from the shocking transformation, Sirabetta had no time to react as Alysha burst from the trees. She shouted and tackled Sirabetta, slamming the tattooed girl to the ground. The *Teacher's Edition* snapped shut and hovered in the air as Alysha tried to pin Sirabetta down.

"Get off me!" Sirabetta yelled. She managed to get free and tossed Alysha aside. Sirabetta quickly looked down at her tattoos and gasped—when her arms and legs shrank down, many of her formulas had run together. They were useless.

She glanced up at Alysha, who had balled her hands into fists. Though exhausted, the girl was ready to fight. Sirabetta looked at her own hands and saw the multicolored spiral— the mark of the Board of Administration—that would let her control the Book.

It, too, had been affected by her younger body—it now spread beyond her palm, missing parts where her fingers spread. It no longer glowed; it was ruined. Alysha, Simon, and Sirabetta all looked up at the Book, which wasn't just hovering anymore. It was vibrating, shaking in midair, as if it was overcome with fury.

Only Simon heard the noise, like a mental snarl from the Book as it surged forward, streaking down and smacking into Sirabetta on the head. She collapsed, unconscious.

The Book floated gently over to where Simon lay and

came to a rest at his side. "Nice shot," Simon said in a pained but steady voice. He wiped his mouth, cleaned his good hand on his shirt, and sniffed. "Anybody else smell a vacuum cleaner bag?"

The Breeze blew gently, dispersing that stink and reviving the kids a little. Alysha sighed with relief and looked around. "Hey, where's Owen?"

"Did we win?" a ragged voice called out from the nearby crater.

Owen's head appeared over the lip of the large hole; he was struggling to pull himself out. "You know, this really-really-really hurts."

Simon and Alysha laughed and broke into coughing fits. Then Simon nodded. "It's over. We did it. We won."

"Don't be too sure about that, lad."

Simon, Alysha, and Owen turned and stared in silent woe. There, standing in the clearing, were Willoughby Wanderby, Loisana Belane, Robertitus Charlsus, Myarina Myashah, and most of the rest of the Order of Physics.

CHAPTER 40

Too Many Keepers

Simon was too weary to sit up, much less stand, so he spoke as loudly as he could from where he lay. "It's not what you think."

"Not what we think?" Wanderby demanded. "What do you call that, lad?" He pointed at the Book. "That's what I call incriminating evidence. And you're not just going to run laps as punishment, I promise you."

Owen pulled himself a bit farther over the crater's edge. "That's not fair! We only found it. Veenie and Sirabetta tried to steal it!"

Alysha lacked the strength to yell, but she managed to

speak clearly. "Yeah, and we saved it from them. You should be thanking us!"

Wanderby stared at the unconscious girl in the black wet suit. When he saw the tattoos on her arms and legs, his face went pale. Then, recovering, he scowled. "Sira–who? Enough lies, lass. You may have held off four of us before, but now you've got all of us to face. You're out of the game."

Simon shook his head. "No way. It's not yours. Book, get out of here! Save yourself. Bring help if you can!"

The *Teacher's Edition* rose several inches from the ground. It had received a command from its Keeper and, free from Sirabetta's control, could act. Once again, the air tore open, and with a *POOF*, the Book disappeared.

A collective gasp rose from the gathered Physics members. "What have you done?" Wanderby roared. "Where's the Book?"

Simon hadn't done anything; he was too tired to use his space–time formula. But he believed the Book was safe.

Alysha reached over and squeezed Simon's hand. "We almost made it."

Simon mustered a smile. "It was a good adventure, huh?"

"Yeah, but it would be nicer if we got to live," Owen said; he'd finally climbed onto the path but was too tired to move any farther.

The air between the kids and the Order of Physics rippled and tore, making a very familiar noise, as the air had to put up with yet another hole opening within it. The *Teacher's*

Edition reappeared, floating in midair and still glowing blue. But this time, it wasn't alone.

There were numerous Books floating near it, each with different-colored covers. A person appeared beneath each Book.

(I gasped with recognition as I looked from one startled person to the next—these were no ordinary people. This was the entire Council of Sciences!)

The Keepers were as stunned by their sudden transportation as everyone else.

Dr. Solomonder Smithodrome, a bearded man wearing a brown corduroy suit, was lying down . . . two feet off the ground, as if he'd been on a couch before being transported. He fell to the dirt with a thud.

Short, neatly dressed, bespectacled Gilio Skidowsa was bent over with a bag of seeds in his gloved hands, as if he'd been in the midst of gardening.

All the Council members (even the legendary, silver-haired Math League Keeper Skyrena McSteiner) were there, ripped from whatever activity they'd been in the midst of before Simon's *Teacher's Edition* summoned them. Skyrena was poised with a piece of chalk in hand, as if interrupted while writing on a chalkboard. She looked around, tugged at her odd conical hat. "Observation: displacement via transverse axis, $d = \alpha\, e^t$. Reference: *Teacher's Edition of Physics*." Her floating red Book tilted forward, as if agreeing with her.

For a moment, everyone stared at black-mustached

Allobero Foreedaman, the Keeper of the Order of Astronomy; he wore only shiny silver underpants. Seeing everyone's stares, he shrugged. "What? I was orbiting Mercury, getting a solar tan." He snapped his fingers and mumbled a command; in response, a tiny portal appeared in the air, spitting out silvery pants and a black, heavy-metal band T-shirt. They moved on their own, dressing Allobero as he stood with arms outstretched.

Wanderby placed his hands on his hips. "Just who in Galileo's name are you people and what are you doing in our woods?"

Gilio looked around the forest. "Dunkerhook Woods. It's been a while." He turned to Wanderby. "We are the Council of Sciences," he said quietly but firmly. "Stop blustering and let us speak to Ralfagon."

The members of the Order of Physics tensed. Most had never met the Council; they were very suspicious after the last Physics meeting.

Simon saw the assembled Physics members on one side and the various other Keepers on the other and shuddered at the thought of a fight between the most powerful beings in the universe, with Alysha, Owen, and him in the middle.

"Wait!" he shouted with his last strength. "I think I can explain."

Gilio looked down at the kids, as if noticing them for the first time. He adjusted his eyeglasses. "Indeed?"

"We don't listen to the enemy!" Wanderby shouted.

The *Teacher's Edition of Physics* swooped away from the other Books and hovered protectively over Simon, Owen, and Alysha. It flashed a bright blue light, and in response the other Books flashed their own identifying colors.

Immediately, the Keepers put hands to their heads, as if concentrating. Their Books were communicating with them.

Gilio leaned toward Simon. "That's quite a story the Books have told, but we'll need proof. Take me to Ralfagon so I can heal him."

Loisana held up a hand. "Wait . . . what's going on here? As far as we know, these children stole our Book and hospitalized Ralfagon."

Simon pointed at the unconscious Mermon and youthful Sirabetta. "It wasn't us! It was them—Mermon Veenie and Sirabetta!"

"Veenie, I could believe," Loisana said, "but I've never heard of this Sirabetta."

Solomonder stepped forward. "*Vas?*" he said with an Austrian accent. "Pardon me, but did you say 'Sirabetta'? This *girl* is *mein* Sara Beth?" He walked over to her unmoving form and looked at her face. Then he rose and nodded. "*Ja*, it is true; I can barely tell like this, but it is she."

Wanderby grew paler and jittery. "No, this isn't right. You're all menaces. Yes, that's it! You're all against us!"

Gilio cleaned his glasses on his sweater. "And they say I'm a conspiracy nut."

"Book," Simon called out, "can you bring Ralfagon here?"

The *Teacher's Edition of Physics* tipped forward, as if to nod, then disappeared in a flash and a *POOF*. It reappeared seconds later with a loud tearing of air. A hospital bed with Ralfagon, unmoving atop it, materialized a few feet away.

Eldonna was sitting on a padded chair that materialized next to the bed. She leapt to her feet. "What? Who? Where?" she sputtered.

Allobero chuckled. "Someone stop her before she gets to 'how' or 'why.'"

Gilio stepped forward and looked her in the eyes; he was the exact height as short, stout Eldonna. "Pardon me, my dear. My name is Gilio Skidowsa." He smoothed his sweater and smiled. "I'm the Keeper of the Order of Biology." He cleared his throat. "I believe I can be of some service to Ralfagon."

Eldonna quickly collected herself. "Gilio of Biology? Yes, Ralfagon spoke of you often. You won't hurt him?"

"I'd never hurt him; he owes me money from our last Council poker game."

Gilio walked over to the pristine white hospital bed and placed a hand on Ralfagon's forehead. "Dislocated shoulder, fractured hip, cracked ribs, moderate concussion . . . and an ingrown toenail. No problem." He whispered a formula, and Ralfagon glowed bright green for a moment. "Done."

Ralfagon sat up, put one hand to his stomach and the other to his head, and gazed into Gilio's eyes. He smiled broadly, clapped a hand on Gilio's shoulder, and said, "And just who are you?"

CHAPTER 41

THE FATE OF OUR HEROES

Loisana groaned. "Oh no! He has amnesia?"

Gilio sighed. "How convenient. You owe me money, old man!"

Skyrena clapped. *"Demonstratum: onustus domus, unum supra octos."* Five playing cards, three aces and two eights, appeared in midair briefly.

Ralfagon's eyes brightened. "Gilio! Good to see you again." He looked around. "Sorry, friend, but I don't have my wallet with me." He looked down. "Or my pants, apparently." He looked up and saw the *Teacher's Edition of Physics* hovering by Simon. "Something's different with my Book. Er, that *is* my Book, isn't it?"

"There's so much to explain," Simon said. He looked at the *Teacher's Edition*. "Can you do it quickly?"

The Book tilted in a nod and flashed blue. Ralfagon put a hand to his head again. "Oh, my. You traveled back in time to the Monday before my attack to find this boy? When I told you to go anywhere or anywhen, I didn't think you'd take me so literally." He looked at Simon. "You've had a busy week, haven't you?"

Ralfagon swung his feet off the bed and paused. "Has anyone seen my cane?"

Allobero snorted. "How many times have you lost that thing, Ralfagon? I swear, it's the last time I give you anything special." He snapped his fingers and another portal opened, dropping Ralfagon's cane beside him on the bed. "Next gift will be an apple; if it was good enough for Newton, it's good enough for you."

Ralfagon climbed off the bed, leaning heavily on his cane. He looked closely at Simon, Alysha, and Owen. "You three are a mess. Gilio, would you mind?"

Gilio tended to their injuries. His formula made them tingle all over, but it healed them painlessly. Gilio then licked a finger and held it up in the air, as if testing the wind. "Do I detect one of my own flock?" He peered around until he spotted Flangelo's prone form. "Oh, Flangelo, this is no time for a nap."

Flangelo glowed green and sat up quickly. "Gilio! You've come for me!"

Gilio patted him on the shoulder. "Yes, m'boy. Apparently, you've learned to be heroic. Well done." He gently healed the fallen sparrows, too.

In the meantime, the members of the Order of Physics warmly greeted their restored Keeper. Wanderby bowed his head. "I guess I was wrong about the lads and the lass." He looked at the kids. "My apologies." He didn't sound sorry at all.

Ralfagon cleared his throat and spoke a few formulas that encased Mermon Veenie and Sirabetta in a glowing blue sphere. "There. They are contained now."

Simon exhaled in relief. Then he looked Ralfagon in the eyes. "Um, Mr. Wintrofline? You know, Sirabetta was kind of psycho, but she did have a point. It doesn't sound like she was treated too fairly before."

Ralfagon glanced at Solomonder, then at the other Council members. "Perhaps the matter is in need of review. Perhaps many things are." He looked Simon in the eyes. "I don't know if you realize just how serious all this is, young man. You and your friends have broken almost every rule of the Knowledge Union. We will be dealing with the repercussions for a long time."

Alysha crossed her arms. "We also saved all your butts from those two!"

Ralfagon made sure his hospital gown was closed in the back. "Oh, that, too. And you have my sincere thanks. Now, I believe the Council and I have much to discuss. And according to my Book, we have a new Keeper to deal with."

Simon gulped. "You mean me?"

Ralfagon nodded. "The Book chose you. It saw something special in you—vast imagination, great courage. A good heart. Even Dunkerhook Woods saw fit to invite you in, despite centuries of keeping Outsiders out. Plus, you live around the corner: location is everything." He coughed. "The Council and I believe that the Books' higher understanding of the laws of reality give them great wisdom, so who am I to argue with the *Teacher's Edition*? Simon Bloom, you have now joined the Knowledge Union. Welcome, Keeper."

The Order and Council members all gasped.

"There's also a short ceremony and a special cake, but we can arrange that later," Ralfagon added.

Before Simon could react, Flangelo said, "Thank goodness, now can we do something about his name? I mean, Simon? Bloom? Hardly Union material, wouldn't you say?"

Gilio shook his head. "Not now, Flangelo."

Simon was stunned, but after a moment, he grinned widely. "You know, I was too busy trying to stay alive to think about what would happen if we actually made it. I mean, how great is that, guys? We get to keep our powers!"

Ralfagon cleared his throat. "Ah, right. About that. I'm afraid your brave friends won't be able to keep theirs."

"Bright side, at least you can keep your names," Flangelo

chirped. Gilio glared at him and Flangelo whistled sadly. "Right. Sorry."

"My apologies, Owen and Alysha," Ralfagon continued, "but we can't let you into the Order without following Union protocol. There are procedures and tests."

Simon looked at his friends, who were clearly devastated by this news. "What if they promise to be careful?"

"I'm sorry; it's forbidden," Ralfagon said. "There are rules we must follow. Don't worry; you two should have no trouble with the tests. If Mermon Veenie passed, anything's possible." He turned to Simon. "I humbly ask that you yield control of the *Teacher's Edition* to me," he said.

Simon turned to Alysha and Owen. "Guys, I'm so sorry."

Alysha and Owen nodded sadly.

Simon looked at the Book, now trembling in midair between Ralfagon and him. "Go on," he whispered.

The *Teacher's Edition* flashed blue, and for the first time, Simon heard its message in his mind instead of having to read from a page. *Thank you, Simon. We'll be together again soon*, it said in a gentle, soothing voice.

Then the Book flew to Ralfagon's outstretched hand and the clasp popped open. Ralfagon gestured and a burst of blue and white sparks leapt from Alysha; the last drop of electrical energy she'd stored was released harmlessly.

"I respectfully remove your formulas, though I still call you friends of the Order," Ralfagon said. Alysha and Owen glowed blue for a moment, then sagged where they stood.

Ralfagon turned back to Simon. "We have much more to discuss later. For example, out of all those laws, you chose space-time?"

Flangelo nodded. "That's what I said, too!" Then he caught Gilio's look and chirped nervously.

Ralfagon sighed. "Terrible things could have happened using space-time; even I don't know all it can do. For now, Simon, be careful. Your powers can cause problems for all of us. Please keep all this secret, even from your father. My work with his research must move at a slow pace, with the greatest care . . . as with all the Union's activities among Outsiders. We have a grand purpose that requires the utmost precision." He paused. "What was I saying?"

Eldonna stepped forward. "Ralfagon, why don't I pull young Simon aside and arrange a meeting during your office hours?"

Ralfagon rubbed his chin. "Office? Oh, right, at that university. Of course."

Gilio cleared his throat. "There's one more important matter, Ralfagon." He pointed at Mermon and Sirabetta. "Those two almost certainly have fellow conspirators in the Union. That means you three may become targets for revenge. Children, you must be on your guard."

Willoughby, standing to the side, was glaring at Simon. On hearing this, he smoothed out his expression to appear unbothered.

Ralfagon rubbed the head of his cane. "I think that's it for now, Simon. The Council and my Order have some business to discuss. But we'll soon figure out what's to come next for you and your friends."

Eldonna gently tapped Simon and handed him a note. "For later."

Flangelo walked over to Simon, Alysha, and Owen. "Looks like you three did okay." He whistle-laughed. "And I managed to avoid getting flame-broiled."

"Hey, thanks for helping out back there," Simon said.

Flangelo sighed. "What can I say? Sometimes even a chicken has to become an eagle." He looked right at Owen, who nodded to him.

Simon, Alysha, and Owen waved good-bye and walked along the trail. "Guys, it could be worse, right?" Simon asked of his friends.

"Worse?" Alysha smiled. "I've been on the adventure of a lifetime. So what if I'm back to using batteries and plugs." Her smile slipped a tiny bit, and she sighed. "Okay, it does suck a little."

Owen nodded. "It would be great if we could keep our formulas or at least be able to play with yours, Simon. I don't know if I'm ready for everything to be so normal and quiet all the time."

"Who are you and what've you done with the real Owen?" Alysha asked.

All three laughed as they stepped onto Van Silas Way in the twilight.

"Anyone for Nezzo's?" Simon asked.

"Then maybe we can go back to Narrator Geryson's place later and watch the fights in replay mode." Owen smiled. "I'd like to see myself in action."

Simon opened Eldonna's note. "Speaking of action, Eldonna says your tests won't be for a while. But she said the woods are pretty much empty every day except Sundays. So if anyone wanted to go there to have fun with, say, gravity and friction . . ."

Alysha cheered. "All right!"

Owen started to cheer, too, but he paused. "This time can you *please* not make me slide on my stomach? If she gets to slide on her butt, I get to slide on my butt!"

"I have a better idea," Simon said. "What if we try sliding, friction free, while standing on our heads?"

"No!" Alysha and Owen shouted together.

"Okay, okay, then what about this . . ." Simon said as the trio walked off together.

FORTUNATELY, I LOVE ANCHOVIES AND BLACK OLIVES

I switched off the Viewing Screen and stretched. Another piece of history concluded and with a happy ending: the children, the Order, and the universe were all safe.

Still, the Knowledge Union was shaken to its core. They would have to come up with new plans to deal with danger to Keepers and threats to the Orders. The Council of Sciences needed to find a way to handle Sirabetta as well as to find her unknown allies and the source of her mysterious tattoos.

There would be damage control throughout Lawnville; there had been more public uses of formulas than ever before. Outsiders might become suspicious, if they weren't already.

Plus, the Union now had two Keepers in one Order for the first time ever. Simon's link to the *Teacher's Edition of Physics* changed everything. The future of the Order (and my work) would be *very* interesting.

I stretched and brought my empty teacup to the sink, reflecting on how my advice had aided the children. I hoped my punishment wouldn't be too harsh.

There was a knock at my door. Could the kids be back already? I glanced at the Viewing Screen. Still off. My Chronicle was over.

I opened the door. To my shock, Miss Fanstrom stood there, holding a Nezzo's pizza box in one hand and her briefcase in the other. She ducked her head under the door frame, and her hair twisted to shut the door behind her.

She marched into the apartment. "Hello, Mr. Geryson, nice to make your acquaintance at long last. Good show overall, and you demonstrated excellent discretion with Simon and his friends." She placed the pizza box on my kitchen counter. "Don't worry; you're in no trouble. There are just a few matters I'd like to go over with you before you next Chronicle a piece of Simon's history. And things I'd like to show you from my Book." She tapped the notebook computer inside her briefcase.

I stared numbly, unsure of how to react.

She looked around. "It's a bit cramped in your flat. Why don't you get dressed so we can go to the park around the corner and eat? Get ourselves a breath of fresh air. I can't have such a skilled Narrator feeling miserable, can I?"

The top of her hair swiveled to point toward the fridge. "Come, now . . . I brought the pizza, you get the soda. I think you've had enough tea today." She gestured with the pizza box. "I just hope you like anchovies and black olives."

At last I regained control of my mouth, but all I could manage to say was, "Miss Fanstrom! What are you talking about? What are you doing here?"

She smiled and pinched my cheek gently. "Tut, tut. My students call me Miss Fanstrom. You can call me boss. Or Keeper, if you prefer."